Men and Angels

Men and Angels

Marc Schiffman

ISBN: 1530844215
ISBN 13: 9781530844210
Library of Congress Control Number: 2016905784
CreateSpace Independent Publishing Platform
North Charleston, South Carolina

C H A P T E R   1

Usually I remain in my room for Christmas. The season brings out people's dreams and despairs in the worst way. For days, they shed their familiar skin. They lose their equilibrium. The animal emerges. In Hong Kong, the cool, rainy season fails to deaden such spirits. On this particular Christmas Eve, the air in my room felt dreary, the whiskey tasteless, and so I ventured outside and joined the thousands on the street.

Standing on the curb of Nathan Road, I listened to the Christmas Eve revelers, the hoots and shouts of teenagers and half-drunk Chinese. A six-story Santa Claus in vibrant neon decorated the front of a department store, and ropes of glowing silver bells stretched from one lamppost to the next. Atop Hong Kong's Hilton Hotel, a large clock worked its way toward midnight, while the surrounding streets, strewn with pedestrians, were closed to traffic.

From the subway portal on Peking Road, a large mass of teenagers burst onto Nathan Road and swept me off the curb and into the street. They drank beer from oversize plastic cups, yelled Christmas greetings and danced wildly beneath glowing neon. Huddled in doorways, mothers harbored their children frightened by the swelling crowd. Within minutes, I was shut in and surrounded by the jubilant faces.

When a reveler began to whistle jingle bells, I looked for an exit. As I turned, I startled a Chinese girl, her arms wrapped around a leather bag that hung bandoleer style across her chest. She stepped backward and slipped on the slick cobblestone street wet from a recent rainstorm. I caught her as she went down to one knee and hauled her up. Her hair was braided in one long, sinewy strand, her cheeks florid from the cool evening air.

To my left, the large hill on Nathan Road, crammed with people, grew noisier. The dense crowd reminded me of the narrow alley in near-by Mongkok, where birds in wooden cages hang from store rafters, and strange winged insects in plastic bags are displayed on tables.

Before we could speak, a wave of people surged forward, and she was pushed to the ground. Wedging my hand downward, I fought for a hold around her waist, but she slipped my grasp. I stood still as the undertow of knees and hips tried to shove me down. When the crowd moved sideways, I was struck in the side of the face, stunned for the briefest moment, as elbows and half-closed fists knocked my head and shoulders. Seconds later the girl touched me on the ankle, beneath my pants, a cold hand. This time I brought her up swiftly.

Above us, fireworks lit up the night sky. With my arm around her waist, I clawed our way through the crowd until we moved out of the street onto the sidewalk. I pulled two terrified boys from a small nook where a vendor had once been, his watch stand demolished, and threw them back into the river of people. We stood flattened against the building's concrete wall.

She glared at me. "Who are you?"

"Sam Merlin."

"My name is Melinda Lin."

A stout girl in a black leather jacket swept past us. Her head and shoulders were above the crowd line. It was as if she were being handed from person to person, a human rag doll whose feet barely reached the cobblestones. She waved a handkerchief in the air and seemed to be chanting words of encouragement. Within moments, the girl disappeared from view, and as the fireworks dimmed people began to fall, slipping on the wet street, struggling to escape like the strange insects I had seen in the plastic bags in Mongkok. Shortly, shouts rang out, and people tried to inch their arms free, digging their hands and elbows into the lower backs and shoulders of strangers in front of them. The weaker and smaller ones in the crowd lost their footing and fell as people fought for an avenue of escape.

My shirttail was out and Melinda's fingernails dug into the fleshy part of my back. Panicked, she kicked me, again and again, her heel hitting the concrete wall of the building, her toe recoiling into my shin. I almost smacked her. Instead, I tried pinning her deeper against the wall. With my body wedged against hers, my hand touched her cheek, but she resisted the caress. I traced the rails her gaze was trained on. A young girl lay on her back, only two or three feet from us, being trampled. I didn't reach for her. I should have, I know this now. But for some reason, I merely stood frozen with expectation, looking down at her.

The girl's eyes were half open, her neck misshapen and partially depressed. She wore a school uniform, a peach blouse and a blue-and-green checkered skirt. The skirt, ripped up the seam and clumsily hiked up on one hip, exposed the white underwear. Her legs were hairless and thin as matchsticks. She had one gold band on her middle finger. A minute later, a boot stepped on the hand, and one of the fingertips split open like a rotted plum.

A megaphone voice neared, and the fatigued crowd thinned and siphoned off onto smaller side streets. I moved toward the unconscious girl, fighting my way past scores of people running for safety. Not long ago, I had seen corpses spread on the frozen ground in Afghanistan. The corpses were young and old, all heavily clothed. I had been on a quest for a client to retrieve an ancient artifact, one of the world's oldest dolls. This child appeared no different from those on that Afghan region.

On my knees, the girl appeared even younger, the forehead unlined, padded with childish fat. I took hold of the blue-and-green checkered skirt and pulled the remaining fragment down, covering her thigh. My fingertips touched the patch of skin where her blouse had been torn while my other hand rested on her hip and, unexpectedly, I felt something give way. The hipbone separated and the unnatural feeling of loose flesh and muscle startled me. Where resistance should have met my hand, I now had the power to push my way inside her. I withdrew my hands and held two fingers to the dead artery in her neck.

A truncheon rapped on a nearby lamppost, and a policeman marched toward me, waving me away from the girl. His young face was drawn and ashen. Several bodies littered the ground, some moving, others quite still. The policeman pointed his truncheon at my nose and shook his head. His legs, dressed in perfectly razor-creased blue pants, trembled. I broke contact with the girl, found Melinda, and quickly left the nearly deserted street.

CHAPTER 2

IN MY APARTMENT, Melinda stood beside the bureau, away from the table lamp. She needed a place to clean up. She removed her black jacket, the ankle-length lavender skirt and long-sleeved blouse. I was surprised by her boldness, the simplicity by which she stripped off her clothing, the way she folded both skirt and blouse and placed them on the back of a chair. She did these motions with experience, as though she had performed this rite before in front of men. She wrapped the towel I had given her around her body.

"Do you believe in Buddha?" she asked me.

"I'm not a Buddhist."

"When such terrible things like tonight happen, you can't grieve. Only accept. This is the Buddhist way."

She opened her purse, removed several paper squares from her wallet and unfolded them, revealing lines of Chinese characters. Later I learned she had been educated in English-speaking institutions, but among her friends she spoke Cantonese.

"Buddhist prayers," she said, holding the paper squares in her palm. "I don't think you can read Chinese. But if you want you can keep them."

She entered the bathroom. Listening to the shower, I gazed at the hand-written black ink characters and placed them in my shirt pocket. Minutes later, Melinda exited the bathroom with the towel wrapped around her. Droplets of water covered her shoulders and arms, and her unbraided hair hung limply down her back. She retrieved her clothes and returned to the bathroom. I stretched out on the bed.

"What are you doing?" Melinda asked.

Dressed, with her hair combed and her arms folded across her chest, she appeared ready to leave, and I wouldn't have lifted a finger to stop her.

"Are you okay?" she asked.

I don't know where the words came from, but when I spoke them I felt neither shame nor embarrassment.

"Would you stay for a while?"

In one athletic motion she lay beside me and rotated her body so that we faced one another.

"Do you see this scar on my cheek, Sam?"

The scar, an inch in length, was a shade paler than her lovely brown face.

She said, "When I was seventeen I was kidnapped by my boss for four days. He cut my cheek with a razor and raped me. I have a baby because of it. I was in the news and on TV, too. I got some money from him, but not much. My son lives with another woman. He's three years old. I'll get him back," she said, confidently. "He knows I'm his mom. I write him letters."

"That's a good thing to do."

"Where's your wife?" she asked.

"I have none."

"And your family?"

"All gone. I live and work in Hong Kong now, not America. I'm a kind of orphan you, might say."

"Why do you say you're an orphan? You're American. I think no one from America is an orphan."

"My grandparents and parents are dead; I have no siblings. I had a dog once, but he ran away with a cat."

She grimaced at my poor humor. "I was raised in an orphanage for twelve years," Melinda said. "I have a few pictures of my mother and some memories. I know nothing about my father. That's a real orphan, a girl or boy who lives in a place without parents and has no memory of love."

"Tell me, where do you usually sleep?"

"I stay in a woman's dormitory at a secretarial school. I take classes at the school. There are many girls. Some are illegal Chinese girls. They'll do anything to stay in Hong Kong. They are like flowers walking across a floor of flames."

"And you're different," I said.

"Yes. I know what I have to do. I have a goal, a purpose."

For a while she studied my face, as if to discover some kindness in me.

"The electric light," she said at last. "Do you sleep with it on?"

"No, never."

"Please, turn it off."

"I need it," I said.

"Why?"

When I had leaned over the girl in the street and went to touch her shoulder, I thought nothing would be dramatically different. She would still be real. There would be the same texture to her skin and on my hand the same sensation of warmth from her mouth before the mob had crushed her windpipe. However, when I touched her I felt the loss of something I could not name, which, in fact, seemed insignificant and was not worth naming. But as I glanced around the narrow and shadowless room, it seemed as though she had followed me, had for some reason attached herself to me, and because of this, her presence that would not leave me, I feared the darkness and needed the light.

"Why?" Melinda repeated.

"It's the girl in the street," I confessed. "She's in the room."

"You should pray for her."

"I can't. I haven't prayed in a long time."

She placed her hands together below her chin. "This is from both of us," she said.

When she finished her prayer I unfastened the top two buttons of her blouse and noticed ruptured blood vessels, where someone had left his coarse lips on this spot of flesh. I kissed her mouth. Her lips yielded, and gently parted, a judgment of hers I never completely understood.

After we were silent for a long time, Melinda stood up, went to the bureau and removed a photograph from her wallet. She stared at it, and when she appeared satisfied, she tucked it away, walked to the bathroom and closed the door, leaving a splinter of yellow light against the wall.

CHAPTER 3

❧

For six years, I lived in this apartment on Hankow Road. I traded in antiquities, mostly rare books and valuable artifacts. Originally, I came to Hong Kong on bequest of an American client. He wished to own a first-edition set of Herman Melville's novels, but more specifically a lock of Melville's hair a Chinaman possessed, with a certificate of authenticity. Once found, the Chinaman, a Mr. Wong, became elusive, disclaiming ownership. Within a month, his tiny shop was consumed by fire.

For weeks I searched for him, but he had disappeared. Rumors surfaced among the few dealers I knew, that he had torched the store to conceal his illegal activities in dope peddling and that he'd had a feud with his brother, a part owner in the business. With the loss of the American client, and with little opportunity at home, I decided to remain in Hong Kong. Prospects, I sensed, abounded. Eventually, due to my deteriorating financial situation and my education in antiquities, the illegal peddlers and buyers in stolen artifacts found their way to my door. Shortly, I became their emissary.

I awoke early, before daybreak. Always a light sleeper, I heard the street outside my window alive with vendors preparing for the Christmas Day sales and the mechanical whine of buses.

Showered and dressed, I paused before Melinda's open wallet on the bureau. A corner of a photograph, the one she had looked at last night, was partially visible. I pulled it out. The black-and-white photograph showed a slim, dark-skinned woman in a patterned dress. Her eyes looked too large for her face, and her hands, thick peasant fingers, were placed one over the other in front of her. In the background, a klong and several flame-of-the-forest trees gave an ancient quality to the print. On the flipside and in faded ink were the words, *Bangkok 1967*. It occurred to me as I replaced the photograph in the wallet that the woman was near death.

I sat on the bed. Melinda's eyes opened, and she placed her fingers against my belly.

She asked, "Can I trust you?"

"Like a brother."

"Then I don't want to see you again."

"You're a smart girl."

She pulled the blanket over her mouth. I couldn't help thinking how young she looked, and I had the first tremble in my soul as I calculated her age to mine and sensed that protective quality a father must have for a daughter.

"Listen, I have to run an errand. I'll return around two. The spare key is on the bureau. I'll meet you here."

"Maybe," she said.

"You're cautious."

"Only to those I don't know."

"Two o'clock. I hope to see you then."

Lily Petz's antique shop was south of Mongkok, a healthy walk that left me sweating as I stood outside her store. The CLOSED sign showed through the glass door. I knocked and entered. In that rarified gloom of artifacts that inhabited most of the floor and wall space, the smell on this day was astonishingly pleasant and aromatic. The waru wood of ceremonial Balinese masks and the *pangkalbuaya* wooden sculptures, which resemble crocodile hide, emitted a strong scent, as well as the ancient bejeweled snuff boxes, stirred awake, I believed, by the rain and heavy air.

"Lily?"

"Back here, Sam."

We sat on folding chairs in the rear of her store, as we often did, where the street sunlight failed to reach. The store was long and narrow. Antiquities gathered from every corner of Asia lined the walls from floor to ceiling. There were god-like statues, stone seals heavily and intricately carved from ancient China, porcelain plates, painted glass bottles, multifarious images of Buddha in all sizes, shapes, and types of metal, ivory bracelets, gold rings, and silver necklaces locked in a glass cabinet.

"You should marry," Lily said, pouring green tea into two cups from a delicate porcelain teapot.

"I once was."

"Funny how Americans slip out of marriage. They're children at marriage. They act on whims. No one divorces in China. Very rarely that is. In Asia, the family is the focus."

"I didn't know you wanted to see me for a lecture in sociology."

"Sociology?"

"The study of human society."

"And what has your allegiance today--love, friendship, money?"

"You have my allegiance as always, Lily, especially when you hand me a mission."

Upon most visits, Lily had some delightful morsel for me to sample, but this morning there were no small cakes or cookies, and even the tea tasted thin and bitter, as if it had been brewed days before.

"There's a package waiting for me in Bangkok, Sam, and I need someone to guarantee the items are genuine."

"Are they stolen terracotta Chinese warriors?" I asked, half-curious.

"I'm not a smuggler like you."

"I'm reformed," I protested weakly.

Lily poured me a fresh cup. The sudden patter of rain rattled the glass door and windows.

"Last night many people were trampled to death on Nathan Road," Lily said. "Did you hear? Nothing like this has ever happened before in Hong Kong, at least not since the war. A shame, all those children."

"I was there."

"And is it true?"

"Yes, a lot of kids are dead," I said.

Lily touched the kettle. "The tea's cold."

She left, kettle in hand. In the rear room, with the door ajar, I heard her humming what sounded like a church hymn.

"I'm getting fat," Lily declared, pinching her arm, standing in the doorway.

"A couple of kilos, is all," I said, and it wasn't meant to hurt, my careless remark, but I saw her grimace, that great Chinese hurt when my response should have been deferential, kind to the point of apologetic.

"I need you to go to Bangkok and to check if these porcelain bowls are legitimate. They're from the Ming Dynasty. I know you've handled goods like this before. I believe you can tell the difference between fakes and authentic bowls."

"I've seen enough fakes. So, don't worry."

"Of course you have," she replied curtly.

"Is it for the shop, or do you have a private client?" I inquired, resisting her barb.

"That's not important."

"And my cut?"

"Ten percent of the net sale price."

"People have been known to disappear for smuggling less valuable items than Ming bowls out of Southeast Asia."

"You sound worried. Why? That's not like you. You've done this countless times. I promise that the fellow you will deal with is not evil."

She was prepared for my question, and the slight venom in her voice was meant to entice me.

"I usually receive a higher percentage for smuggled goods," I said.

"Very well, I'll give you fifteen percent. There's always the unknown factor."

"Yes, the demon factor."

That someone will get pissed off and use violence. I'm a pacifist at heart. I haven't clubbed a person in a long time. I'm wifeless and childless and that tends to make a man like me withdraw from the world and avoid violence because, in the end, I know no one will come to my rescue.

"I've never misrepresented myself or my aims," Lily stated. "I've always told you the truth."

The kettle whistled, and Lily exited. I wanted to call to her but didn't. Instead, I peeked around the corner. Lily stood running her fingers over her rotund hips and belly the way a lover might. With an air of distress, she dropped her hands and stayed this way: a heavyset woman disappointed with her body and a person, me in this case, whom she thought was a friend and not an enemy. I returned to my chair.

The shop was her home. A cot was setup in the rear room where she sometimes slept. She reminded me of one of the blanc-de-Chine figurines she kept locked behind the glass cabinets, a translucent porcelain with a thick glaze, beautiful but afraid of the open air.

When Lily came back, she held a book in one hand a plate of sandwiches in the other.

"Page sixty-one shows a picture of the Ming bowls and the address of the man in Bangkok who's keeping the bowls for me. His name is Mr. Sunthorn."

I took the book. Lily placed the sandwich plate on the table. She wore fresh lipstick, and I detected a wisp of perfume. At one of our first meetings, Lily had removed a small, green crystal bottle shaped like an artichoke heart from her purse. She had withdrawn the stem and moved the tapered tip, moistened with the saccharin scent, from behind her upper lobe and had made a line to her collarbone and had repeated the same ritual with the other ear. I never made an advance. One time, I believe, and the memory is vague, after we had left a restaurant, and beneath a sultry moon, I kissed her cheek, or meant to, catching her black hair flying across my lips as she fled toward her apartment. I smelled of alcohol. It had been my birthday, a melancholy day for me.

"Well, will you go to Bangkok, Sam? You never answered me."

"Anything for you," I said cheerily.

"When will you leave?"

"In a few days."

The wind had escalated, and heavy raindrops fell loudly against the windows.

"Please," Lily said, "eat a sandwich."

I ate three and took the book with the pages marked that concerned Lily's Ming bowls.

As I stood in the street outside her shop, I saw her framed in the large glass door. Her freshly painted lips looked distorted through the streaked glass, her face as noble and tortured as the Balinese masks on the shop walls. She waved once and flipped the sign to OPEN. I had the odd feeling as I strode away that she had failed to tell me something of importance.

CHAPTER 4

ON FAT KWONG Street the Liu brothers, Zhi and Yi, picked up my scent and followed me with a casual air. Zhi nodded at me when I glanced back. I moved at a steady pace and was not surprised when they stood beside me at Wo Chung Street. They looked like marionettes, as if a stiff elbow crack to the sternum would send them to the pavement in a heap. Zhi was juiced, his flat eyes deader than usual, but Yi, shorter and a bit stouter, bumped me with his shoulder. I looked down, and his hand was balled in his brown leather jacket pocket, as if to hint he held a small caliber pistol. We stood beneath the awning of Lee's Noodle Shop.

"Talk time," Yi said.

"I have to be going," I replied.

"It's about the doll. The old one."

"I prefer my girls smart and young."

"Wise-ass American," he said in Cantonese.

Before I could respond, Zhi popped out of his lurid world and said, "Afghanistan."

Yi nodded. "We have a buyer. A lot of money is involved and some will fly your way."

"I no longer have the item in question."

"Sure you do," said Zhi. "Mr. Wong told us. Remember him? You burned his shop down, you crazy arsonist. He's relocated but still active in the trade and told us about you and the doll."

"He's as transparent as China's Politburo. Don't believe a word he says, friend."

Zhi rotated in front of me and half-smiled, exposing an upper row of crooked and stained teeth. He could have been a handsome boy if not for that dirty and twisted maze of enamel. Poor hygiene, it's always a sure sign of an untrustworthy artifacts dealer. His smile withered. He said, "Kamaldeep."

Ten years ago, in Kabul, I killed a man. I had been driving a car fast and a tire blew. My colleague, Kamaldeep, and I spun off the road, into a ditch, and collided with a tree. Kamaldeep flew through the windshield. We had been celebrating our find, one of the world's most valuable dolls, by drinking black market wine. I checked his vital signs, but he was dead. I removed the doll from the car and left him in the ditch, beneath an iron sky. I had walked no more than ten meters when I saw bicycle tracks on the pavement. To my right, in the ditch, were the bicycle and the rider. He was dead; his head had been nearly sawn off his shoulders. As we spun, the car's rear end must have smashed into the bicycle, catapulting him off the road, killing him. I walked the eight kilometers back to the city. I didn't contact the police, or Kamaldeep's wife, and left the country on the next available flight.

"Once again, I don't have the item you want."

"But you have its twin. That's what Wong told us. Right?" said Yi, bumping his brother aside, who stood very close to me, his foul breath exceeding the disgust of his teeth.

"Yes, the twin, of course," I grinned. "I'm going to Thailand soon. I left it there in safe keeping. My *key* money, you might say."

"You rascal," Yi said, popping a short left into my shoulder. Zhi joined him and whacked me in the belly with a weak fist. "We'll sell it for you without a problem. We have buyers already lined up. You'll be a wealthy man afterwards. Trust me."

"I'll see you when I return," I said, and left them leering at each other, Yi tugging on his sparse mustache hairs and Zhi blinking his eyes, trying to orient himself to the empty space I'd recently occupied, where I imagined exploding positive ions glowed in his mind's eye after my departure.

Inside my apartment, I found Melinda sitting lotus style next to the telephone. Her cheeks were ruddy, and she smelled of outdoors. There was a phone call, she told me, she had to make, but she had to see the look on my face first. I don't know what look I had on my face. I was wet and cold and slightly scared because it had been a long time since anyone had waited for me, and an even longer time since someone had depended on me and what I said.

She dialed the director of her secretarial school. In a meek voice, she informed him why she had been absent from the dormitory last night. After a lengthy silence, she hunched closer to the small table, politely ended the conversation, and cradled the receiver.

"He called me a whore. I'm sure I can fix things."

"He sounds like a bad guy."

"Not really. He's angry because he thinks I have a boyfriend. He once liked me. How was your meeting?"

"I have to go to Bangkok soon. It's a job for a friend."

"Will you stay in Hong Kong until New Year's?"

"Yes. By the way, do you know you talked in your sleep last night?"

"I do that sometimes. My mother once tried to write down what I was saying, but I woke up because of the way she smelled. I think it was her perfume. She smelled of jasmine. It's one of the few memories I have of her."

I pointed to Melinda's wallet on the bureau and asked, "Is the woman in the photo your mother?"

She nodded. I thought she would turn angry since I had invaded her privacy, but she appeared calm. It was as though a door had opened for me to walk through.

"She died or disappeared. I don't know much about her. The last information I have is that she was in Thailand." She shrugged her shoulders. "She left me. But that's my business. What are you thinking?"

"I was just thinking that if things don't work out at school you may want to go with me on my business trip. It would give you the opportunity to find out information about your mother."

"Someone may get hurt if I go with you. I can't be responsible for you."

I smiled. "I can take care of myself. "

"If you say so."

She rose and tapped the left side of my chest with her palm, the spot where she thought my heart resided.

CHAPTER 5

THE NEXT EVENING a thunderstorm erupted in Hong Kong. The rain bounced off the sidewalk with the explosive force of firecrackers. Melinda and I took refuge in a small noodle shop. We sat by the windows. Melinda ordered for both of us.

"When it rains like this," Melinda said, warming her hands around the hot bowl of noodles, "Hong Kong seems like a foreign country. It's like we're the only two people in the city."

"We aren't quite alone," I said, noting the crowd inside.

"I know. But you're the only one I see," Melinda said. "You should laugh more. Your face looks good when you laugh."

"I laugh all the time. I'm a regular hyena. Sometimes my belly hurts from laughing. I've been kicked out of restaurants for laughing so loud."

"A regular hyena, you say. And what kind of animal am I?"

"A bird."

"Oh. And what bird is that?"

"You're a sparrow because here you are nesting with me."

"You're wrong. I'm a canary bird like so many of my sisters in the dormitory who are locked in cages." She looked out the window. "I don't like living in the dormitory. I don't like it at all. All the girls ever talk about is escaping through a boyfriend or marriage. Chinese or foreigner, it doesn't matter. And some even talk about hurting themselves."

"They'll survive."

"Maybe."

"They will."

She gazed at me for a long time, and the wonder I had seen in her eyes changed to one of placid acceptance, as if I were simply another warden who had imprisoned her into a different cage.

Afterward, Melinda returned to her dormitory and I went to a local bar. The rainstorm had passed, and though it was a weekday, the bar was nearly full. I removed Melinda's prayers from my pocket and perused them. I wanted them to inform me of her nature: I wished to spy on the invisible universes she occupied.

At a far table, lit by a greenish Carlsberg wall sign, Lily Petz sat with a fat Chinese gent. His large arm rested on her shoulders, and she seemed dwarfed by his fatness. He wagged his finger at her face and he spoke loudly to her, but when she tried to shrug off his arm, he pulled her back toward him. I walked over.

"Hey, Lily."

"Hi, Sam."

"How are you?"

"Fine."

"And you?" I asked, directing my remark to her fat Chinese boyfriend.

"Go away," he said.

I took a sip of my beer. "That's not very polite. Well, let me buy you a drink. What are you drinking? Ah yes, beer. And you, Lily, what would you like?"

"I'll talk to you tomorrow, Sam."

I raised my beer to toast. "Come on, man. To long life! Lift up your mug!" He glared at me and spoke in Cantonese to Lily. I understood a sizeable portion of the Cantonese language. "No, my man, I'm not drunk you, silly bastard. I just want to toast. You can do that, can't you?"

"Are you nuts, Sam? This is my boyfriend, my fiancée."

His mouth turned into a mammoth half-moon and he squeezed her.

"He must be from a wealthy family. Otherwise, why would you want to marry such an oaf?"

Lily looked away, and her boyfriend threw his beer in my face. It was warm beer; he must have had it in front of him for a long time.

"My new shirt," I protested, and before he could reply, I threw my beer at him.

Accidentally, my beer glass slipped out of my hand and cracked him in the forehead. On his feet, he lunged for me across the table. I skipped backward, out of his reach, and slammed into the men behind me who, in retaliation, pushed me into the hungry grasp of Lily's boyfriend. Surprisingly nimble for his size, he put me in a chokehold; I kicked him in the knee, leaned backward and hit him in the cheek with a roundhouse punch.

We tumbled sideways like two punctured helium balloons and landed on the floor. With his arm locked across my nose, I shoved my elbow into his belly, once, twice, and tried to gain leverage by arching my back. He spun me onto my belly, belched loudly, and with all my might I rammed my elbow into his ribs. He halted and moaned. Wiggling free, I scrambled to my feet. Behind me, someone slapped me hard on the back of the neck. Turning, I looked for the assailant but only dour Chinese faces greeted me. No matter how long one lives in a foreign country, the residents given the opportunity easily vent their cultural nepotism. When I turned back, Lily was on her knees, massaging her hero's head.

"What are you doing?" Lily yelled out.

"I thought--"

"My fiancée! He's my fiancée! I don't need rescuing!"

"Is our deal still on?" I inquired.

"Yes!" she screamed at me.

On the street, a mist covered the streetlamps. Neon store signs were lit, and there was the rakish smell of Victoria Harbor.

I realized that I had been in the wrong. Initially, I had thought Lily was falling into an abyss, but it was I who had slipped, taken myself one rung lower, into the second circle. For quite a while it seemed I had been moving headlong toward trouble.

"We've decided to go with you to Thailand," Yi said, standing outside my apartment entrance. Zhi, wearing a maroon beret, leaned against the brick wall, rubbing his nose and the small hairs on the bottom of his chin.

He continually shot his right index finger at me, as if trying to send a telepathic message.

"What's wrong with Zhi?" I asked.

"He misses you."

"Touching."

"Mr. Wong said you're not to be trusted, so we'll go to Thailand together and snatch the doll."

"*L'Oiseleur.*"

"What?"

"That's the dolls original name. It's a four-foot-tall automaton doll with sword, flute, pair of singing birds, and fancy Renaissance-era clothing. The doll plays the flute, *Marche des Rois* by Georges Bizet. It's run by spring-driven cogs and gears."

"Are you kidding me?"

"Screw satellites and the Internet. This doll is wizardry."

"Man," Zhi said in dismay, "you're coming apart at the seams."

This time the telepathic right index finger had been transformed into a .22 caliber pistol. Zhi jammed the barrel against my belly. Beneath the brim of the beret, Zhi's slit eyes resembled a Komodo dragons steely gaze, a species perilously near extinction.

The BMW was at least fifteen years old with the front seat covered in fake lambskin. The heavenly aroma of lemongrass from a plastic cube scented the air. Zhi, seated behind me, as if in jest or joy, poked the pistol barrel into my neck.

"Don't do anything crazy, Merlin. I've got you. Got you in my sights."

"Tune it down," I said. "And where are we going?"

Yi said, "A friend of Mr. Wong wants to meet you. A Russian defector. He's the guy interested in the doll by--"

"Some genius."

"We're thinking of cutting Wong loose if this new fella works out, and if you pass his inspection."

"Do you think there are really wizards and witches?" Zhi asked from the backseat. "It sounds like only a wizard could make this doll from five hundred years ago. You're a troll, Merlin. Only a troll could get his hands on something made by a wizard. Do you know what we do with trolls in Hong Kong? We burn them. But you know about burning. You did a good job on Wong's house of business. Have you ever burned anything else? Anyone else? Fire is kinda electric. Once it gets under your skin it's like meth, hey, it whispers in your ear, hey, it murmurs *lick me, eat me*." Zhi wrapped his bony arm around my throat and placed an open clear cylinder next to my nostril. "Take a ride." His sinewy forearm tightened on my throat. "Go ahead, Mr. Troll, take a couple of deep sniffs."

"Love too," I said, and did.

Zhi held his forearm against my windpipe. "Another draft," he said, "just for laughs. A meth trip. Nothing beats it."

The old BMW's shocks rolled sweetly and seductively with the dips and valleys in the road; the sky was bluer than I had seen in a long time, and a white veil similar to the ones I had seen brides-to-be wear in Afghanistan drifted in the eastern region of sky.

"Let's take him to the whorehouse on Tai Woo Street," Zhi said.

"This is a business trip," Yi said. "Get out of your lunar landscape."

"Escape? Okay, why not."

Zhi placed the pistol barrel hard against my neck and did figure eights with the meth cylinder until he plunged it into my right nostril. I did the job, once, twice, three times, and then the .22 went *pop* into the car's roof. We lurched from one end of the road to the other until Yi hit the brakes and we settled in a narrow ditch. Zhi was in a fetal position in the rear seat. Yi reached over, seized the pistol, and struck his brother two times on the ear, hard, solid whacks that brought tears to Zhi's eyes.

"Five minutes and we'll be at Heifetz's house," Yi said to me. "Five minutes. Let Zhi whirl away for a while, but I need you coherent."

"Trust me. Say, what's the asking price? Tell me, cause if I know I'll jack it up for you. I know this doll's history and how many lives have been lost trying to get it and sell it. There's one story about this seventeenth-century pawnbroker and his broken-down mistress. The pawnbroker's wife was bedridden with gout, and his mistress would roll five, six sailors a night for enough cash so that she and the pawnbroker could buy this doll from another pawnbroker who had no idea of the doll's value. And once they had the doll, they'd sell his business, feed the wife horse piss to worsen her gout, and then light out for Paris. Of course, the whore was usually drunk by the third or fourth customer, and she was often rolled by a sailor near the end of the night, so—"

"Shut up," said Yi.

"That's good shit."

"You're deranged."

"No argument." My nostrils were numb and I felt a flowering, pristine valley rise and bloom in my forehead. "Did you say Heifetz?"

My father took me to Carnegie Hall when I was ten. He was a failed violinist and sold cars instead, but down deep, in a core of him that I never quite understood, music stirred, its creative breath wheezing like a phlegmatic dipso. He never could discharge the ghost. I don't know if it was love or jealousy that drove him to take me to Carnegie Hall that late autumn evening. I had no interest in music. But Joseph Heifetz was his favorite violinist. I recall, a year later, in a drunken rage when my mother left him for an anesthesiologist, he played every record he owned by Heifetz, and broke each vinyl record after he had listened to both sides. Then he took a hammer to my bicycle. It was the one thing I owned that I prized, and he knew it.

So, imagine the surprise when Yi and I waltzed up the brick path, rang the bell, and a man who looked exactly like Joseph Heifetz opened the door. He was the spitting image of the man I had seen that autumn when I was a kid. A violin bow was tucked in his armpit, and a rope was looped round his waistband, holding up his pants.

"Yi, is this da scoundrel who has the doll? Well, come in. Come in. We have too much to talk about, young man."

We sat down in teakwood chairs that smelled of antiseptic. My high had flattened out. It puffed out on the edges of my vision, tickling my gums, providing me with a false sense of security.

He looked at me. "Do you like music, Mr.—"

"Merlin," I said. "And, sure, music is cool."

"My uncle was Joseph Heifetz, the famous violinist, and I'm just Heifetz the Russian defector."

"You don't look like your uncle."

"Tie him up, Yi."

With alacrity, Yi bound my wrists with duct tape to the chair. I hoped he wouldn't place the tape across my mouth.

"This is so you know that I want what you have and I'll take all steps to obtain it."

"I believe you."

Heifetz winked at me as if we were collaborators. "He doesn't believe me, Yi."

Yi stripped off my belt. Heifetz waltzed up to me. He was surprisingly nimble for a man of his age, and made G clef notes with his bow against my privates. I could smell the rank odor of his body. He hadn't bathed in days, it seemed. His hands and arms were covered in grey, coarse hair, the knuckles on his right hand that held the bow overly large, as if they had been broken in a bar fight.

"Was your uncle truly Joseph Heifetz?" I asked.

"Yes. He used a silver wand Tricolore gut G string and a Goldbrokat steel E string medium including clear Hill brand rosin. Heifetz believed that playing on gut strings was important in rendering an individual sound. Who else would know this kind of junk?

"There's a story about my uncle dueling Itzak Perlman with bows at Carnegie Hall. They fought who had the richer, warmer tone and who better expressed the use of *portamento*. The story has gone from hearsay to legend to fable. Heifetz, the tale goes, won by clubbing Perlman over the head with his cane."

"So, how much will you pay for the doll?" I asked.

I had grown weary of his speech and smell. My high had evaporated, and I was left with a raccoon splitting headache. Heifetz hovered closer to me, within inches. Spit flew from his mouth as he talked.

"I'll check the doll out first to make sure it's legit. But I'd guess around a hundred thousand dollars U.S. for you."

"Cool."

Then Heifetz slapped my face. Almost immediately I felt a welt form above my right eye.

Heifetz said, "In Petersburg, when I was a young Russian agent for the KGB, I witnessed an interrogation. I think she was a Pole. Usually this kind of interrogation takes months. The KGB were methodical. First, you build a rapport, like I am with you Merlin." Heifetz grinned. "But the best way to get information and cooperation is called the Breaking Method. The most important part is to make the person talk by telling him that you want simply to understand. Then you tell him we can find the way to deal somehow with the situation, which is not very bad right now. Do you understand, Merlin?"

"The clouds are parting."

"I think you wouldn't last very long under torture."

"I don't know. My first wife did a good job on me for years, and I just took it, with a smile."

Heifetz folded his arms. Yi taped my legs to the chair. There is something very unpleasant about being tied to a chair. It reminds one of distasteful dreams of being buried alive and the true inadequacy of words to save oneself.

"The person, of course," Heifetz said, "will lie to you. But it doesn't matter. What matters is that he's talking, or in the Pole's case, she's talking. I listened to the interrogator question the Pole. After a minute or so the interrogator would review her story and next break her story down into short scenes. Then he started interrogating her on each scene but not in any chronological order. After a couple of days of this, and with little sleep, she was frantic. Just worn down. It's pretty hard for a person to keep lying if you act like this. Everyone, Merlin, has a breaking point. Indicators are when the person leans forward and his facial expression hints of an interest in the proposal, or he is more hesitant in his argument. Then he is nearing the breaking point.

"But the Pole was tough. This surprised me. Courage. Fear. The same bag of worms, most times. If you believe that I have swamp land in Florida you might be interested in buying. Her story remained untranslatable. Several guards eventually raped her in the cell. And pulled out her fingernails. She babbled like a drunk then. Most of it was the truth. She didn't know much about her organization."

"What does this have to do with me and the doll?"

"I trust you to deliver the doll to me. Otherwise, you'll be in the same position as the Pole. Boxed up and shipped to a foreign zip code." Heifetz brow wrinkled. I was a dissident chord in his orchestra. "Cry, boy," he said. "I wanna see you cry."

Zhi swaggered in from the doorway and stood behind me. He draped his right arm across my chest and plunged the meth bottle into my nostril. I was tired of this trip and yanked my head away, but Yi clamped his hand on my jaw.

"Having fun, Merlin?" Yi asked.

I inhaled many times. The room swooned. I heard laughter and violin music, the sound sweeping over my body in a barren caress.

Was it Zhi or Yi who cut my bonds, planted a kiss on my cheek, and whispered a line from the Lord Buddha *To understand everything is to forgive everything*? We left down the serpentine path. I recall the halo moon in the upper right quadrant of night, vaporous, as if it were able to lift itself from orbit and vanish.

Outside my apartment door, my key ring had tangled up with my pocket threads. Exhausted, I yanked on the ring.

"Careful Sam, you'll break the key off in the lock acting that way."

Melinda sat on the floor in the shadows, her arms around her knees.

"I thought you were going home."

"I'm not ready for a confrontation with the director." She stood up. "You look like hell."

"I was kidnapped, put in jail, and molested with a violin bow."

Melinda took the key from me and opened the door.

"Are you drunk?" she asked.

"No. Not even close." The apartment smelled musty and needed airing. I opened the two windows in the living room and flicked on the ceiling light. "I wasn't actually tossed in jail. I was kidnapped and tied to a chair."

"Tied to a chair? Then you should get drunk. As long as you don't go crazy, maybe you need to get drunk, maybe you're funnier drunk. I'm trying to find something nice to say to you."

"I would never have guessed you had a mean streak," I said.

"All caged birds have claws."

"Are you thirsty?"

"Tea would be nice."

I placed the teapot on the single burner. After the water boiled, I poured the green tea into two mugs, added whiskey to each, and sat in a chair.

Melinda pulled her sleeves down over her hands to hold the hot mug. "You're a handsome man. I bet you have a lot of girlfriends. But that's not what's important to me."

"And what's important to you?"

She put the mug down on the floor and touched her breast. "Men think this is important, or your sex. But what counts can't be seen."

"Is that what I need to understand?"

"It's something you have to learn." She stretched out on the bed. "Hey," she said. "I just want to sleep and not worry the director will come over to my bed. He's done that before. In his slippers, he'll stand beside my bed, kneel down, and put his hands on me. The last time I yelled at him to stop he ran away, but he'll come back. There's something about me that intrigues him. I don't know what it is. The other girls are prettier."

"Maybe it's your rebellious nature."

"No. Chinese men like girls they can control. He knows I have a child and that I was raped. Maybe that's what makes him desire me. He thinks I'm helpless. But I'm not. I know how to get what I want."

I removed her shoes and retrieved her tea.

"For months after I was attacked," she continued, "I took my shower in the dark. No lights. I couldn't stand to look at my body. I disgusted myself. I wouldn't let a man into my sex. But in my ass, I thought that would be okay, but it wasn't."

"It's hard to forget evil times and evil men."

"Yes, but easier than one thinks. An old woman told me that truth. She'd been in Nan King China in 1936 when the Japanese came and slaughtered everyone. She was a teenager. The Japanese raped her, beat her and left her for dead, but she lived. I see mostly good now, and I remember the good things in my life."

Melinda shed her jacket and pulled the folded blanket at the foot of the bed up to her collarbone. She sipped her tea. When she finished, I placed her mug on the table and took off my shirt and pants. She lifted the blanket and I lay beside her. Like the stripping of sun-burnt skin, the eighteen years difference in our age peeled away and did not exist. A distinctive peppermint scent came from her hair.

"Do you know anyone in Thailand?" I asked.

"Not a soul."

"Then where will you begin to look for your mother?"

"The bureau of records. I know my mother's maiden name. I believe she was married to a Thai man."

"And if that fails?"

She closed her eyes. "Something else will come along. It has to."

CHAPTER 6

SINCE ARRIVING IN Asia, I had made love to several Asian women and had lived with a couple of others for varying periods. With each new affair, I was reawakened from a lethargy that had seized me for weeks or months on end. Perhaps this lethargy was due to my travels and dealings in possessions from the dead. When in America, this malaise had been worse. I barely ate and lied whenever I needed to obtain an artifact for a client. I moved like a sleepwalker, feeling nothing and caring less. It was only when leaving the states and establishing my home in Hong Kong that an emotional revival occurred.

On my first journey outside the states, at the age of twenty-three, I lived in a one-room shack in a small Mexican town. The Spanish language came easily to me, as most foreign languages did. My room had adobe walls and a hard earthen floor. The cool January breezes made the room tolerable for sleep in the evening. One night, after drinking for hours in the local cantina, celebrating what I believed was a startling archeological find from the nearby mountains, my neighbor saw me peeing in the bushes. He was a poor laborer whom I admired due to his loyalty to his wife and his daughter, Cecille, who had planted Triumph Tulips next to my door.

"What are you doing?" he screamed. "Why don't you piss in the outhouse like everyone else?"

I waved affectionately at him, and he laughed. At night, birds sang and someone banged a drum from one of the nearby shacks. Men and women sold food from street stalls, tacos and burritos with spicy green sauce. Often in the evenings, I read books by the glow of the ceiling's white bulb.

For weeks, the Mexican people ignored me. *"Oh, that crazy Americano,"* I'd hear them say. *"He sleeps with all that broken pottery and the voices of the dead."*

I became known in town, not for my rowdiness or lewdness or carryings-on in the town brothel. I was the foreigner who went into the mountains alone, where the demons, according to legend, lived. Even the bandits avoided this mountain region, making my passage easier. Eventually, my room grew fatter with old clay pots, shards of ceramic, bullet casings, teeth, bone fragments, arrowheads, and rock carvings. For months, I journeyed into the Sierra Madre del Sur Mountains, spending days camped and searching for relics. One day, on holiday in Mexico City, I bought a record player, a box of records, and brought them home. For many of the people on my street, this was the first time they had heard jazz, and the seductive voice of Etta James.

"Hey, man," one of the neighborhood kids said to me. "Play rock n roll."

I did, but afterward I played Chet Baker and John Coltrane and told the small group of boys the beginnings of jazz. Beneath a yellow harvest moon, I also explained that their mountains were jazz mountains because they held the origins of their people, culture and ancestry. The boys laughed, smoked weed, and jabbed fingers into my arm and ribs wanting to hear the latest American tunes.

One late August afternoon, upon returning home from the mountains, I discovered the door to my room ajar. Window glass and broken artifacts covered the floor; the player and records were missing. I stepped outside into the sunlight and sat down on a wooden crate.

The laborer, who lived two doors away, ambled up to me. He brushed a fly away from the tulips. "The police did this. It's good you were not here, amigo. They were looking for you. I don't know why. But you'd better run." Before I could protest he said, "Don't be loco. They are dangerous. And if you stay you'll vanish. Poof."

"I like it here. My work in the mountains is important."

"This is not your home. You're not Mexican." He spat into the dust. "You are a good boy. It's not worth it to die in a Mexican jail. You're poor. You can't buy your way out."

"Why are the police after me?" I asked.

He laughed. "You're American. They see you stealing from our country. Even if it's junk pottery. They want you away. That is all and that is enough. There are no laws when the law can be bought. You have no rights here. I feel a little bit sorrow for you and that is all." He turned and gazed at the crimson sun above the mountains. "Understand that the law only considers hate and greed and revenge. Most of the world is ungodly." He stared at me. "I tell you as a friend now to go. You are a boy. Maybe you will know more as a man and maybe not."

He wiped the sweat below his nose with his shirtsleeve and walked away. An hour later, with my bag packed, I took the Greyhound bus north to the border. As the bus driver throttled up on the highway out of town, and with the window down, I swear I heard one of my jazz records being played at high volume.

Staring at Melinda, I wondered what my Mexican neighbor would think of me living in another foreign country, still collecting artifacts from forgotten eras, embracing the dead and trying to forge a bridge into the past that was more vapor than reality.

Sometime in the night Melinda had removed her shirt and pants. Beneath the blanket, her skin felt chilly. It was as if my body understood her place beside me before my heart or mind did. Her thigh moved and nestled my groin. With her fingertips, she fluffed the soft hairs of my chest. She was silent and only the movement of her hands revealed her impatience.

I seized her hips and slid inside of her. With her breath on my face, it seemed as if she wanted me to see through her eyes, feel with her spirit; instead I shoved these things away, fearing possession and yet knowing I was already possessed by her.

I pushed her up, the blanket fell off her shoulders, and she leaned backward, resting on her palms. Mouth open, she stared at the place the two of us were joined, and when she found the electrical arc in her body intensify she reeled forward. We rolled onto our sides. Her breath quickened. I finished aggressively, taking her tongue in my mouth, gripping the nape of her neck. She coughed afterward, and I noted red marks on her throat where my fingers had been pressed.

C H A P T E R   7

IN THE MORNING, the day before New Year's, I dropped a large cloth bag onto Melinda's dormitory bed, untied the drawstring and pulled open the neck. The girls of the dormitory gathered. They spoke rapidly in Cantonese to Melinda, but a couple directed their words to me, happy to practice their English.

"How are you, sir?"

"Fine."

"Where do you come from?"

"I'm American."

"Oh! Amereecan! We like Amereecans!"

They were younger than Melinda. I looked at their fresh faces, the brown skin of their calves below their long skirts, and the way a few held hands. Melinda had informed me that some of them smuggled boys and soldiers into the dormitory and that others had children of their own.

Melinda placed all her clothes, books, small boxes, and letters on the bed. As the girls delivered question after question, I could think only of this woman beside me, somber and quiet, dropping all she owned into a laundry bag. I knew then, as I do now, I would have done anything for her, committed murder, if she asked.

With her possessions packed, I drew the string taut about the neck. Melinda said a few sentences in Cantonese to her friends. The sepia light from the windows shadowed the posters of rock idols and movie stars taped to the wall. We walked down the corridor. Melinda, as she passed, touched the folded-back mattress of an empty bed.

"This was my friend's bed. She disappeared one night and never returned."

"Listen," I said. "I'd like to buy you some new clothes before we leave."

"All I want is a black leather jacket."

"You won't need one in Bangkok."

She stopped before a half-full basin on a table near the dormitory exit and stared at the concrete wall. A nail head was still visible in the concrete from where a mirror had once hung. She put water on her face, on her hair, into her mouth, and forced it down. I could do nothing but watch and, for an instant, I was back in that Hong Kong street on Christmas Eve waiting for someone else to intercede.

"You're right. I don't need a black leather jacket. Bangkok will be hot. You're very kind to me."

I handed her my handkerchief. She took it, dabbed her throat, and pocketed it. Her face was still wet, with water streaking her hair and making her look, as she walked out the door into the windy air, as though she were on fire.

For New Year's, I wore a new silk tie, the multicolors blending perfectly with my favorite blue shirt and with Melinda's aquamarine blouse. We both wore black slacks. She seemed pleased that we had dressed alike, as though we were brother and sister.

"I wish I had your white skin," Melinda said, feeling the hair on my arm.

"And I wish I could be as dark as you so we could lie on the beach all day in the hot sun."

"I want a big nose like yours."

"But I love your flat nose," I told her and gave it a gentle squeeze.

"Don't touch," she said with a smile.

"Your breasts are beautiful," I said, opening her blouse.

"They're small."

"No, they're perfect. And your lips, too."

"Please, stop. I know I'm not pretty. But you're a kind man to tell me."

She buttoned her blouse and grabbed the box of candy that she had bought as a gift for her godparents', Aunt Maya and Uncle Bernard, whom we were to visit.

We left Kowloon and took the eight o'clock Star Ferry to Hong Kong Island. But instead of going directly to her godparent's residence, Melinda took me to a small garden near their home where tomato plants three feet high were staked and tied with strips of cloth. Marigolds huddled along the perimeter. The small garden appeared well maintained. Melinda entered first, and in the heart of the garden, she crouched before a rotund Buddha and an urn that lay on its side between an opening in the vines. She prayed silently, lit a joss stick, and placed it before the Buddha.

"My brother Caesar," she said, gesturing toward the urn. "I wanted to show you before we left for Bangkok. I don't know what to do with his ashes. Auntie Maya told me it's a sin to keep them for so long. It's been a year now. He drowned. What should I do with them?"

I turned from her, trying to distance myself from her religious posture. Just beyond the garden cars passed noisily in the street.

At first, the weight of the urn thrust into my chest shocked me, and the moist soil encrusting the urn felt like old meat.

"What are you doing?" I said.

"You take care of Caesar," Melinda said. The front of her blouse was sprinkled with dirt, her hands, her cheeks, the bottom of her chin, too, as if she had lain on the ground beside the urn or had smothered it with kisses.

"Melinda, I don't want this."

"Excuse you," she said.

"What?"

"I give you this like my body, my heart. This is a part of me, too. My brother, Caesar, is the last of my family."

"You have a son, don't you?"

"Let's not talk about that."

"Is that a lie?"

She rapped on the urn with her knuckles. "Hello, Caesar. Hello. This man will take you now." With a half-smile, she repelled my resistance. To Melinda it was as if I carried a newborn in my arms, our child, and not the remains of one long dead.

"It's okay with Caesar," she said, stroking my arm.

I held the urn away from my body; it was heavy, the article itself, I thought, not the body of ash. The urn was made of metal.

"You don't know what you're doing," I said.

"I trust you." She bent down, picked a tomato from a vine and sniffed it. "This will taste good." Then with a dirty finger she marked my cheek. "He's not really dead, you know, not your kind of dead. He has an afterlife."

I lowered the urn against my belly. She expected more of me, I realized, than I imagined possible for myself, and I retreated a step, awed by her devotion to her brother.

With the urn in my hands, I exited by the little gate. Hefting the urn against my shoulder, I glanced back and watched her until the decline of the sidewalk swept her from sight. I walked for blocks, feeling the strain in my arms and lower back.

Near a sandy section at the Tathong Channel, I heaved the urn outward and saw it momentarily spiral and splash into the tranquil black waters. Caesar rested now with the bones of his ancestors. Unbuttoning my shirtsleeves, I washed my hands in the water.

Melinda stood on the upper portion of the road and called to me, her voice motherly. "Is there a problem?" She approached through the stiff grass, and when I faced her she said, "I'm sorry if I made you mad. I don't want you to change your mind about us. But I'll respect your decision."

"Nothing's changed, except now I know about Caesar. Are you all right?"

She looked out at the channel. "I would have chosen the same place."

Across the bay, the lights of Kowloon burned, and in the channel the Star Ferry slowly faded from view. From that distance, it was difficult to distinguish the people onboard from the black water. We climbed the slope up to the road.

Before we reached the bus stop, I pulled Melinda aside and handed her an aquamarine stone shaped as a horseshoe, my good-luck charm for flying.

"Here," I said. "This is for you. It's gotten me safely round the world many times."

She took the horseshoe and held it tightly in her hand. "Mine?"

"It's yours. Tomorrow's plane had only one seat available. I've made arrangements for you to fly the day after tomorrow." I handed her an envelope with the airline ticket and some cash. "The hotel address is inside in case we miss each other at the airport. I thought we would leave as soon as possible."

She nodded, looking grim, and removed something from her key chain.

"For you."

She put the object in my hand.

"It's the year of the rat, Sam."

I dropped the plastic, pink rat into my pants pocket.

"Fly safe," she said, and kissed me on the mouth, beneath a street lamp, two lovers, and so it must have appeared to passersby, with their whole lives ahead of them.

CHAPTER 8

———— ❧ ————

AT NOON, MELINDA arrived at the hotel by taxi from Bangkok's Suvarnabhumi International Airport. Due to a detour at Chatuchak Market, where nefarious dealers congregate awaiting comrades like me to sell or buy their semiprecious items, I had been unable to meet her. A short, swarthy man exited the taxi first. He put his arm around Melinda's waist and lifted her up onto his hip, as one would a child, and carried her across the shallow stream in the street. It had poured furiously an hour earlier. Now water overflowed the gutters, reaching the wheel wells of cars. The street water hit the man's ankles, as he deposited Melinda on a dry step. He returned to the cab and retrieved her suitcase. He whispered into her ear, his hand squeezed her arm, and touched the lower part of her waist before releasing her.

I witnessed this from the hotel's café window. She lingered after the taxi departed, then stepped down into the brown water that covered her shoes. I met her at the hotel entrance.

"Who did you come with?" I asked, as we approached the front desk.

"I came alone."

I requested my room key and took Melinda's suitcase. We walked up a single flight of stairs. The hallway windows were open and the heat and late afternoon sun filled the wide clean space. The stone floor tiles shone a pale radiance.

Once inside the room I said, "I saw you with a man."

"Oh, him," Melinda said. "We shared a cab."

"You knew him."

"He helped me. That's all. I didn't know where to go. You didn't meet me at the airport."

She slipped off her shoes and sat down in a chair, sighed from exhaustion, and from her pocket removed a small beaded purse. She undid the purse's string, pulled out my horseshoe, and jiggled the bag so I could see that something else weighed it down.

"All my money," she said. "It's for you."

We slept at the Hotel Opera. The smoky evening light of Bangkok passed through the curtains, making the darkened room appear like early morning, drowsy and warm. Outside I heard the rumble of a *tuc-tuc*. A woman passed our door speaking in Thai. To our west flowed the serpentine Chao Phra Ya River. Its muddy waters hummed with late-night ferries, and along its riverbanks stood modern multi-story hotels dwarfing the dilapidated tin shacks, homes for the poor. The river, smelling of fuel and sewage, carried junks, old swan-shaped boats and sleek, motorized ones. Monks in pumpkin-colored robes with shaved heads and wooden beggar bowls boarded ferries and rode with natives and foreigners alike. Linking arms, the Thais formed human barriers for the monks, ensuring them safety from contact with any female.

Two days after our arrival, we spent the afternoon in a long-tail boat cruising the Chao Phra Ya River and its winding outer estuaries. Houses, built on wooden stilts, lined the quiet banks. We often cruised with the engine cut, on Melinda's request, to listen to the birds and the sounds of the province. On the river, boats stocked with fresh fruits and vegetables pulled alongside houses and sold their goods to barefoot women in colorful sarongs, squatting and bargaining with the seller, while boys bathed and shampooed their heads in the murky water.

One time, Melinda splashed the young crew. She screamed as they returned the barrage, and as the boat rocked from our laughter we drifted away upriver to the boys' exuberant shouts in Thai. Drenched, Melinda stretched out on the boat's bottom. Why do I remember that afternoon so vividly? I recall the pitch of her laughter on the river, her breath tangy from a mango she'd eaten, the way she'd lain in the bottom of the boat, her black hair soaked from river water spread against the red wood, and the wet hand that reached out and held my bare ankle.

In the evening, we dined at an outdoor restaurant beneath a gray sky.

"What do you want to eat?" Melinda asked, showing me the menu.

"Grilled prawns."

"Also *kaeng phet kai*," Melinda said. "Curry that makes you sweat."

"And to drink?"

"Singha beer," she said.

She ordered. The Thai man scribbled on his pad. Melinda smiled at me, her teeth bright against the dark skin of her face.

"You're lovely," I said.

"What did you say?"

"I gave you a compliment."

"Yes, I know."

She wore a sleeveless summer dress, sandals, and a gold wristwatch.

"Are you sure you want to sit here?" I asked. "It's very hot. And we've been out all day."

We were alone on the outdoor terrace. The other customers sat behind large glass windows in the refrigerated restaurant.

Melinda glanced at the windows. "I'm sure."

"Why?"

"I like it," she said.

"Are you afraid of them?" I asked, gesturing toward the windows.

"I'm all right."

She said this matter-of-factly, but I knew she felt threatened by foreigners. Usually she preferred taking her meals in the hotel room or, when in Hong Kong in my apartment.

She removed a pocketbook from her handbag and began reading. On the cover were a boy and a girl in a loose embrace, the characters drawn like ones on American romance novels with lithe, athletic frames and thick hair.

After a few minutes I asked, "What's it about?"

"It's a romantic story."

"Is it good?"

She looked up. "Yes," she answered and returned to the book. I glanced over the lip of the book at the Chinese characters that meant little to me.

"Can you read it to me?" I asked.

She exhaled and put the book aside.

"Please, don't stop reading."

Her thumb flicked the pages. "You want to know the story? Okay, I'll tell you. There is a girl who is engaged to marry a rich Chinese lord. She is poor and not beautiful but pretty, I think. She doesn't want to be poor anymore. So, she tells herself she loves this lord. And maybe she does. But there is another man, a teacher, and he is poor, too. One day when they are finished with the lesson at the school house, she walks him to the road that leads to town and his small room over a shoe shop. When he sleeps, he says to her, he smells leather, and if he has a bad dream he smells the bad odor of feet that slide into the shoes. The sun is setting, and the road is getting dim, but there is still enough light so the teacher can see her face and she can see his. He is handsome, but he has no money. She hands him flowers. So your dreams will be sweet-smelling, she tells him, and he kisses her. She does not stop him. He kisses her many times. He pauses and, unable to speak, he runs down the road. She goes home and prays. The next morning the Chinese lord comes to her room."

She placed the book into her handbag. Her voice was flat, almost glum, embarrassed. "I don't know the word in English," she said. She grimaced, placing a fingertip to the bridge of her nose. "--Spies. Is that the word? Yes. The Chinese lord has spies. He knows about the teacher. Soon afterward, he gives money to the girl's family as dowry, a large sum that sends them to their knees in gratitude and respect, far more than she is worth, they believe. She marries the Chinese lord. She has a baby. And the teacher dies."

"How does he die?"

"He drinks carbolic acid."

"I thought the story would have a happy ending."

"I haven't finished the book. Maybe it will. Maybe it won't."

"What do you think will happen?"

She shrugged. "Who knows?"

"Guess."

"I can't."

"Are you upset?"

"Why, no. I'm happy," she said with an arched eyebrow. "It's only a pocketbook story."

During the meal, the story remained in my thoughts like a wheel I could not quiet. At last, I poked the heart of the wheel and touched the hate in me. It happened quickly, the transference of love to hate, and I thought then that love and hate were one body. But I know now they are two seeds, halved by passion and fear. I believed, at that time as well, Melinda held an equal devotion for her Buddha god and me. Perhaps it was my sudden awareness of this, how these duo forces slept serenely within her, side by side, that angered me, stoked my anger as I fought her Buddha god for greater claim of her affection.

At the end of the meal, I said, "If I die in Thailand, that would make a sweet little tale. A romantic story you could tell your girlfriends when you return to Hong Kong."

"What are you talking about?"

"The death of the teacher. That's me, isn't it?"

"You are a crazy man," she said. "Life isn't a pocketbook."

"What do you know," I said harshly. "But that's exactly what life is. People's lives ruined by girls with secrets."

"Why do you talk like this?"

"Give me the book."

She grimaced. "No way," and grabbed her handbag, continually pinching the metal latch with her thumb and forefinger.

"I want to read it."

"You can't read it. It's Chinese."

"Give it to me!"

For a second, she almost relented but continued the frenetic action on the bag's latch, as though pulling at an unwanted hair. Then she got up clutching her handbag, walked away from the table and down the bustling sidewalk.

She returned within a few hours to our hotel room, a single gold leaf stuck to her blouse sleeve. She had been to a nearby Buddhist shrine, had prayed, and had bought many gold leafs and had placed them on the body of the smiling Buddha.

Later that night, while she slept in bed, I removed the pocketbook from her handbag. I contemplated its destruction as I stood in the bathroom before the raised toilet lid. The paperback was an oracle and if I destroyed the book, I would end its influence. With the back of my hand, I flipped open the book and could envision the pages ripped and floating in the bowl, the foreign characters swirling as I flushed, sweeping away the barrier that separated us. Language, words, people, I saw them all as relics that held no meaning.

I rifled the book. In the middle of the romance, folded over so they were not visible by their edge, were two letters. I was tempted to tear them to shreds as well: letters to a lover or former lover. How many others were there, I wondered.

The letters were addressed to Tommy Lin Stevens, the envelopes stamped and unsealed bearing a street address in Hong Kong. I removed the letters from the mauve stationary and unfolded them. They were unscented, and that pleased me. One was dated three months ago, and the other was ten days old. The letters were motherly, caring, and sentimental. But there was a section in the second letter that seized my attention.

Last week a sad thing happened to a friend of mine. A soldier was with her in our dormitory room and he was very drunk. He was talking loudly and saying crazy things. We told him to be quiet because we did not want to get into trouble with the director, but he went on raving. When she couldn't keep him quiet, they went into the bathroom. The girl told me days before that she loved this soldier, but I don't think so anymore.

A little later, she screamed and I went to investigate. I won't tell you more, but I called the other girls to help and some did. We grabbed our brushes and steel combs, went into the bathroom, and we hit him and slapped him and he got bloody and ran away.

My friend slept with me that night. I told her to be strong, like I am strong without you. I do not talk about you much because I feel if I do I will lose the magic of you, like giving up a part of your soul that is mine since I am your mother and I carried you inside me for nine months. She cried on account her heart was broken, and I told her all hearts break but do not crumble if we are strong and have faith in Buddha. But the next day I heard she was gone. Perhaps she ran off with her soldier. Two days later an old man, her uncle I learned later, dressed in black, the sign of mourning for a Christian, which she was, came and took all my friend's belongings. She had learned her boyfriend soldier was married, and she jumped into the harbor and drowned.

My boy that is the dark side to life, the part I never want you to know, that I protect you from, and that I hope the lady Rose will never tell you about. Unlike the way I remember my mother, I want you to see me clearly, and this will be possible one day when we are together.

If you wonder about my mother, your grandmother, I do not remember her very well. The things I do remember are few. I can not tell you exactly what she smelled like but sometimes, and it can happen anywhere, I'll smell a flower or someone's washed head of hair, and then I'll think of her. But I don't want you to remember me like that, as pictures fading in your head as they are in mine.

Also, you should know this. If anything bad should happen to me, I write to a man in Thailand for years, ever since I discover a Thailand address in my mother's things, the few possessions I have to remember her. Sometimes he writes to me and tells me stories of my mother in his letters. When I read his words about my mother it is like looking into a mirror and wondering who I am.

Often it feels as if she is alive. I've been told that she left me and is dead, but no one knows how she died and where she is buried. However, what's important is for you to remember I am here for you in this life and the next and always.

She wrote gracefully with each word neither straying above or below the dimensions of the page line, using little o's for dots over the i's. She'd drawn a rabbit in the lower right-hand corner. I sniffed the letter and wished her scent was on the page, as if I could capture a part of her that eluded my detection. But there was only the dryness of the paper, the black ink, and the sorrow. I folded the letters ensuring the proper crease, inserted the letters into their envelopes, placed the envelopes into the book, and returned the book to Melinda's handbag.

CHAPTER 9

"LET'S GO TO Jim Thompson's house," Melinda said, tossing the Bangkok guidebook to the floor-, lit by morning sunlight. Jim Thompson was the famed silk entrepreneur who had mysteriously disappeared in 1967 while on a visit to the Cameron Highlands in Malaysia. His unique home was now a tourist attraction known for its fabulous antiques. "It's funny, but when I look at his house in the book I think I remember it from my childhood."

She sat on the bed as I finished dressing.

"What do you mean you remember his house?" I asked.

"I can't explain. But after looking at the pictures of his house I feel like I've been there before. It's as if a memory picture in my mind has faded but still touches something inside me."

"Were you born in Thailand?" I asked Melinda.

"I don't know where I was born."

"It doesn't matter. You can find a home in any country," I said.

"But it does matter where I was born," Melinda said, getting to her feet and picking up the book.

I tried to take the book from her. It seemed as if I was constantly re-possessing something of hers.

"Wouldn't you want to know the place you came from?" Melinda asked.

"I do know," I said, relinquishing the guidebook, "and it doesn't change a damn thing."

"Well, it's important to me."

Around noon, we took a taxi to Petchbouri Road. Strolling onto a quieter side street, we walked beneath a brick archway and entered a pastoral courtyard that surrounded Thompson's home. Inside the compound were several large flame-of-the-forest trees and a manicured garden. The street noise was gone, and a provincial air hung over the grounds.

There were five of us in the English-speaking tour group. We left our shoes outside the house and walked barefoot on the polished wooden floors. Melinda moved through the house, enchanted by the splendor, lingering in each room, attentive to the guide's tales of Jim Thompson. Occasionally I heard the other guide, another Thai woman, two or three rooms ahead, conversing in Japanese.

The house, constructed of century-old teak walls, had narrow staircases and mahogany floorboards. Pegged to the walls were ornate tapestries. An immense crystal chandelier illuminated the drawing room and a tiger skin covered the drawing room floor. Porcelain, bronze, and stone figurines and bowls from Cambodia and China were preserved behind glass cabinets. The roof tiles were from the ancient Thai capital of Ayuthaya, and built into the walls were black-and-white Italian marble panels from one of Bangkok's nineteenth-century palaces. Thompson's bedroom was the most spartan room in the house. It held a small bed, a rectangular waist-high box, and on the shelves, Burmese figures from Amarapura.

The day was sweltering. The windows in the living room and bedrooms that faced the klong were screenless. It was too hot for the mosquitoes who, when visible, buzzed and swooped drunkenly in the air.

The tour group moved on, but I remained in Thompson's bedroom waiting for Melinda who had lagged behind. I sat on his bed. A moment later, she entered and pressed her hand on the mattress.

"It's hard," she said.

I patted the mattress for her to join me. She did, and I kissed her mouth, embracing her. She pulled away and went to the other side of the room. "Someone might see," she said.

"All the better. Come here."

She shook her head and stared at an open-faced wooden box three feet tall with a maze of tunnels which ran from top to bottom. I rose and stood next to her.

"One-channel television," I said.

"I don't understand."

"You drop a mouse in the top and watch it wind its way through the maze. I guess it was one form of entertainment on a dull evening."

She traced a finger along the box's upper edge. "I wonder why he never married."

"The guide said he entertained many famous women."

"Maybe he liked dancers better. Have you ever been with a bar girl or to one of those special houses?"

Her forehead was beaded with sweat from the high temperature.

"I don't want to talk about this," I said.

"But have you ever gone?"

I turned away from her. It was as if her questions were returning me to a familiar place, like the Afghan plain where I had witnessed many dead, a region I had no desire to revisit, and one that left me unsure of myself. "There are massage parlors," I said, "clubs or just bars in Thailand."

"Like in Patpong and along Sukhumvit," Melinda said, stepping up beside me.

I swatted and killed a mosquito that bled in my palm. I knew if she kept talking I would reveal a corrupt passage from my past.

"Maybe you'll take me to one of the bar shows."

"I don't think I could," I said. "You'd go down there with me, see the girls or a show, which are nasty, honestly, girls pulling strings of flowers and other things out of their vaginas, and you'd find things boring and quite sad for the girls. And then you'd look at me and see me like all the other guys down there, looking to get laid."

"And you think I see you different now?"

"I hope so."

My fingers moved through her black hair, and I felt the sweat and its weight against my hand. I thought she would know without my saying it that those spirits in the chambers of her heart were beings without substance. She shook her head, shaking my hand free.

"I trust you," Melinda said. "It's okay if you have other girls. It's your business."

"There's no one but you, and there will only ever be you."

"You're a smooth talker. I bet you've had a lot of practice."

In the final room, a small, windowless building separated from the main house, Thompson had created a gallery of paintings collected from artists from various parts of Southeast Asia. Standing by the door, the guide mopped her brow with a silk handkerchief.

"All fees and donations," she said, "go to the School for the Blind. The tour is over now."

She smiled graciously, pressed her hands together into a heart shape, a Thai *wai*, below her chin, and exited, bowing as she passed the image of a huge stone Buddha in the courtyard. The group stayed for a few minutes in the sauna-like room.

Melinda touched my hand. "I'm going to the toilet," she said.

Outside in the courtyard, beyond the small building, I went to the brick wall that overlooked the klong. For a moment the world seemed serene, the gently flowing klong near my feet, the rustle of a daring breeze in the flame-of-the-forest tree and against the nearby spirit house, whose power is considerable according to Buddhist philosophy. In front of the spirit house, a girl knelt placing the daily offerings of food and flowers.

On the klong, a monk glided past in a pontoon.

"Pardon, but are you American?"

I looked to my left. "That's right."

The stranger placed his hands on the waist-high brick wall. Immediately, I recognized him. He had arrived with Melinda at our hotel.

"I like to practice my English," he said.

"Sure you do."

"Is this your first trip to Thailand?"

"No."

"Life just a few kilometers beyond the district is much different. It's more like the old ways. This house still lends itself to that way of living."

He abruptly pulled his hands away from the wall.

A line of large red ants scurried along the top of the brick wall.

"Damn," he said, swinging his finger up and down like a ruptured thermometer. He rubbed the finger and held it out for me to see. A red pimple had sprung to the surface.

He said, "I knew a man who was bitten once by an insect, and the next day he had a lump the size of a golf ball on his forearm, and the day after that his whole arm was three times the normal size. Nothing worked. He tried antibiotics, Chinese herbal medicine, and not even the mystic, or the *bomoh* as he's called, from his own village could save him. So they cut off his arm. A simple bite. Maybe it was a red ant, a flying gnat, or a bedbug. No one knew. Of course, a bite from a snake like a habu will kill you. You never know in Southeast Asia what might happen to you, or how you'll be stricken."

"I'm sure you'll survive."

"Longer than you," he said, his black eyes staring at me.

At that moment, someone whistled in our direction. He turned and gave a round-bellied man a curt nod. "I must be on my way, my friend."

"Good luck," I said.

He departed with a brief salute. After knocking a few ants from my pants leg, I left the brick wall and stood just beyond the arches of Jim Thompson's house. Within moments, Melinda came bouncing in my direction, holding several postcards. She stood in the spotted sunlight beneath a flame-of-the-forest tree looking temporarily refreshed.

"You never did tell me," Melinda said, "if you ever went to a brothel in Thailand."

"I have been."

"Was it a long time ago?"

"Yes."

"And how old was the girl?"

"Young," I said.

Melinda pivoted and stood in front of me. Her voice was full of hurt. "How young? Eighteen? Was she as young as eighteen?"

A leaf of sunlight swayed back and forth across her brow.

"I think younger."

"Did you feel sorry for her?"

"No," I said, and that was the truth. I had enjoyed our time together, and had returned days later for another joining and later sat with her on the portico near the rear of the building overlooking the Chao Phra Ya River. I bought her a Coca-Cola. Her name was Pim. We conversed in broken English and Thai. And when she gestured with her ivory-brown arm for us to go inside again to one of the many rooms, I refused, shaking my head and ordered up another Cola. When Pim finished her drink she rose and indicated with her eyes she had to return. Before she left she asked me the name of my hotel. Hotel Opera, I told her, and she gave me a polite *wai* attesting to the hotel's moderate status, and an elflike smile of wonder that struck me with immense longing at that moment. Immediately, I knew I wanted to help her, send her back home and pay for her education. I was a novice then: I was caught in the old savior scheme. I was twenty-four and possessed by a dark lonesomeness and the belief I could do such things that mattered and could alter lives. I watched through the window as she took her seat beside another girl, one among twenty, waiting for the next customer behind a glass wall.

"Was she your girlfriend?" Melinda asked.

"No."

"She liked you," Melinda said.

"I was just another man to her."

I told myself Pim possessed only a working girl's affection. I think that way now. This deception is my armor against her sex, the adolescent love that once swept through me so violently, and the threat she now poses in this older man's eyes: memories of a spirited girl and a voice like so many others I can no longer bear to hear.

"Maybe she was scared," Melinda said, taking my arm and adding sympathetically, "or bored. Being a girl like that can be a boring life."

CHAPTER 10

❧

IN A RESTAURANT on Rama I Road, we sat drinking coffee with Melinda's picture postcards spread on the table before us.

"I saw someone I know," Melinda said, sweeping the postcards into a pile. "A Chinese man from the tour."

"The same guy from the taxi when you arrived at our hotel," I said.

"We spoke a little bit in the taxi. He scared me. I think he's here in the restaurant."

"How do you know him?" I asked. "Besides from the taxi ride and the tour, is there another time that you met him?"

Before she could reply someone called out a name and I saw Melinda flinch. "Carmen," the voice repeated, "we've been waiting for you."

I turned and stared into a fat belly. Then I looked into a chubby, oily face and said, "Beat it, man."

"My friend would like to talk with you," the cherubic man said. "You saw him at Jim Thompson's house. Some kind of family connection he says."

"That's not my name," Melinda said.

"I don't care what you call yourself."

"My name is Melinda."

"We'll be waiting in the rear of the restaurant," the cherubic man said. As he left, the fat belly bumped the back of my chair.

"I should go over, Sam."

"Who is he?"

She shrugged and looked at me. "I don't know the fat one, but it's the old guy who knows me."

I was tired and didn't want to play their game, nor act the unwitting stooge. Though playing stooge was a mask I had used before in unfriendly artifact transactions. It takes humility and a degree of cowardice to play the stooge, both traits I had cultivated for my trade. Probably the older Chinese gent was the one Melinda mentioned in the letter to her son. He was the man with the Thai address, a phantom out of her past who possibly had the knowledge to unravel the whereabouts of her mother. I left the picture postcards on the table, a hopeful sign that we would return shortly.

We found them in an empty section of the restaurant. When we approached, the older man stood, seized Melinda's hand, and shook it vigorously. He had placed a bandage on his swollen finger. We sat down.

"My name is Mr. Wang," he said. "That's what your mother called me. Or just Wang. I knew you as a little girl. And this is John Primo, my nephew. That's not his real name. No Chinaman would have a name like that. He thinks the name Primo makes him sound dangerous, like a drug lord." Wang winked. "But now it's Melinda, not Carmen. Ah, but what's in a name? A dream, is all. It was one of your gifts. You were always a kind of child-changeling. But Yvonne was my favorite name. I think you started calling yourself that at age three." He sat rigid in his chair, his hands clasped on the table. "And you are?" he asked, addressing me.

"Sam Merlin," I said. "Surely you remember me from Jim Thompson's house?"

"Of course. Are you her husband? Her boyfriend? Well, what does it matter to a woman with so many names? Am I right?"

"Did I call you uncle?" Melinda asked.

"You did."

She frowned and said to me, "I had many uncles growing up."

Wang wore a gold bracelet on his right wrist and a pinky ring with a red jewel.

"Melinda, I knew you as a child. But first some coffee. Hong Kong's coffee is dishwater compared to Thailand's." Wang flagged down a waiter and ordered. After the cups arrived, he said pleasantly, "Let me tell you a story. One day I was having tea with your mother here in Bangkok. She was always gentle with you. Though there were times, I swear, when I would have taken a whip to you. You could be a wicked little thing. But she never hit you."

His cheeks turned ruddy from some image, I assumed, from which he found joy.

"Your mother had been washing the floors in Jim Thompson's house when I came by this day. You must have been four years old. She was a handsome woman, especially for a Chinese. So often she was down on her knees, scrubbing the floor. A shame, really, a woman so attractive working like a servant. Oh, do you recall the chandelier in the drawing room?"

Melinda shook her head.

He leaned closer, and I could see his crooked yellowed teeth. "It's not important. Your mother brewed some tea and we sat together in the small living room. While we were talking we heard a scream from the kitchen. A wail really. Do you recall, Melinda?"

"No, Mr. Wang."

"You were wearing blue, skimpy shorts."

"I don't remember."

"Somehow you'd fallen into the metal bucket, toppled it, and the hot water spread all over the kitchen floor. We found you on the floor, sitting in the hot pool, crying. And the left side of your leg, the upper thigh, was scalded."

Melinda touched her leg. At night, I never asked her about the thick scars that meshed with the smooth skin and ran in swirls and valleys on her upper thigh. She had the power to separate herself from her body; she hinted at this feat of hers the time she told me about the man who had raped her and had fathered her child.

"After a day I was no longer there," she had told me. "I was tied to a chair or tied to his bed, but I wasn't there. I was inside here, my head. A thousand miles away."

"And me?" I had asked her. "Are you with me?"

"Completely," she had replied.

"We stripped off your shorts and underwear and bundled you up in a sheet," Wang said. "We raced to the doctor. Your mother had to put a special ointment on the burn for weeks and bandage your thigh every day. I used to watch her. You cried the first day and never after that. Even after your leg began to swell and scab over, you never whimpered. It must have hurt. I'm sure it's still scarred. I know about these things. I was a medic in the army." He touched her fingers. She pulled her hands away and placed them in her lap. "Your mother often wondered if you would ever have a husband because of the scars. She had perfect skin. I look at you, and I see your mother. You are similar in many ways. The eyes are the same. Your body resembles hers, too."

"Mr. Wang, was my mother pretty?"

"It's time we left," I said.

"Your mother was beautiful. When I saw you I knew it wasn't mere chance."

"Yeah, a real stroke of luck," I said.

I knew of their communications. The taxi ride wasn't coincidence; Melinda must have arranged it. Perhaps she had even coordinated this soiree.

"We are colleagues of Jim Thompson," Wang said in a gentler voice.

"Thompson's dead, Mr. Wang," I said.

"That's what everyone believes. But I know where he is, and why he disappeared. He's quite alive."

"Like Elvis," I said.

"Ah, Mr. Elvis Presley." He wagged the bandaged finger at me. "Now listen to me. I played chess with Thompson last week. He's a chess master. He lives north of here. He didn't die in the Cameron Highlands. Folk tales, that's what they are. Yes, the Cambodian Communists kidnapped him, but they didn't kill him. They liked him. He had often entertained many Cambodians in his grand home in Bangkok when he lived there."

With a butter knife, Wang drew two eights on the table. "I believe that's how old he is, but he's fit and alert, except for some gallstones which are bothersome. I'm a reputable person. A school teacher. Surely you remember Melinda? There's a college near Surat Thani. I ran the history department." Wang paused. "Thompson likes Chinese girls, like your mother."

Melinda's eyes widened. "He knows about my mother? Where is she? Sam, have him tell me, please."

Wang asked, "Would you like to meet Jim Thompson? He's still a wealthy man. He could reclaim his house, his business, all he owns if he wanted."

"He believes in charity," Primo added. "You know all the profits from the house tour help the blind. The guy's a true humanitarian."

"At least tell me her name," Melinda begged.

"Your mother was called Madame Wong or Chung Lo-Yu."

"Is that why Thompson disappeared?" I asked. "He wanted to give everything he owned away?"

"Not at all," Wang answered. "After his kidnapping from the Cameron Highlands by a renegade Cambodian group, he convinced them not to ransom him. He didn't want to go back to his old life. He was an unhappy man. So he sold some jewels and antiques he owned through a Mrs. Mangskau, an old friend in Thailand. He knew she'd keep his secret. His legendary parties had become tiresome. He'd become what he detested in others--an icon. A celebrity without purpose."

Primo spoke in a hushed voice. "Thompson is a coward, miss. He deserted his companions, all his friends."

Wang interjected good-naturedly. "He's a man following his bliss."

"A 60s hippie," Primo said disgustedly. "A fucking misfit."

"Thompson is a complex man," said Wang forcefully, "who wanted his freedom. He still has great wealth. He likes me and trusts me. As I said, we play chess together."

"Are you really his friend?" Melinda asked.

"His only one," Wang said merrily. "And I want you to be with me, both of you, when I visit him again. I want to show you the northern hills of Thailand."

When I moved to take hold of Melinda's hand, she flinched and pulled away. Her fingers, I saw, were curled as if they were a receptacle to something strange and welcoming, a loving touch more intense and selfish than mine.

"Melinda, will you come with us?" Wang asked.

"And Jim Thompson," I said. "Where exactly is he?"

I confess I wanted to know more. I wanted to bury him in Melinda's eyes and the illusion that Thompson could be of help.

"Not far from Ubon Province in northern Thailand," Wang said. "He's a Buddhist monk. He preaches the song of flowers and trees; he disdains silk, the foundation of his empire."

"Can he help me find my mother?" Melinda asked.

"Definitely," answered Wang. "We'll leave in a week. All four of us. Thompson wants us to pick up a few supplies for him. He'd be delighted to meet you."

Melinda reached into her handbag and thrust a photograph of her son into Wang's hands. Wang glanced at the front and back. There was Chinese lettering in blue ink on one of the edges, his age perhaps or the date it was taken.

"Why, he's lovely. But he could be anyone's boy. He doesn't look like you. Will you take him with us?"

"He lives with another woman."

"All the better," said Wang, dropping the photo on the table.

"I want you to have this," Melinda said. "I want you to know that I'm more than a name, whatever name you call me, whatever face you think I'm wearing. I'm more than some *thing* to own. I'm no longer that child who fell in the bucket of scalding water. I want you to see me for me. Melinda Lin."

"Of course, dear." Wang rose and Primo followed. "What hotel are you staying at?"

I told him.

"I'll be in touch."

He bent down and kissed Melinda's cheek. Her head lowered. Wang had forgotten to take the photograph, and I placed it in my pocket. We sat in silence in the wake of their departure, the two empty chairs having created a temporary vacuum between us.

"Now tell me, do you remember him?"

"I think so," Melinda said.

"Was that story true about falling in the bucket? Is that how you got those scars?"

"Yes, I was burned. But I don't remember how. I've blocked it out of my brain. I was very young."

"So, he could have invented that story and the one about knowing you when you were a child."

"But where could he have found out about the scars?"

"Perhaps he got the information from a girlfriend of yours or someone at school."

"Why would he go through all the trouble?"

"He wants something from you," I said. "He hasn't told us everything."

She took my hand in hers, and I willingly believed the lie that she didn't fully remember him or the cause of the scars on her thigh and was appeased when we returned to our hotel room and Melinda, after undressing, was first in bed. The ceiling fan turned; the afternoon sunlight fell through the windows' bars in a familiar hieroglyphics. Our bed had been freshly made and our breakfast dishes cleared. Her slender, naked body and her lineless face gave me the impression of her youthfulness, a deception I believed all too heartily, and that I forced easily and blindly upon myself with the same vigor as the belief in her unwavering love.

CHAPTER 11

⁓

AFTER DINNER, WE returned to our hotel room. Melinda curled up beneath the blankets. The picture book she had bought at Jim Thompson's house was open in her lap. She reviewed each photograph carefully. When she came upon a photo of Jim Thompson, she flipped the book around for me to see and announced this man could be her father.

"I'm leaving," I told her, "to meet Mr. Sunthorn. He has Lily's Ming bowls. I need to check them out tonight before he sells them to another dealer."

"You have time," she said. "No need to rush off. Do you think we look alike?"

I looked at the stern, unkind British face.

"No, not at all." I slipped on my shoes. "I have to go to Sunthorn's house. Lily wants the bowls, and I need the commission."

Melinda looked up at me. "Don't be long, darling."

A half hour later I rang the doorbell on Mr. Sunthorn's house. The door creaked open; the hinges were well worn. A bony egg-shaped head, illuminated by a yellow bulb in the entrance, slithered into view. A blue vein corkscrewed from the top of his forehead to his nose.

"Mr. Sunthorn. I'm here for Lily Petz's Ming Dynasty porcelain bowls."

He had allowed enough room to squeeze his elongated head through the door opening.

"I don't know you, sir," he said.

As he retreated and inched the door forward, I slammed my hand against the hard wood. The sound echoed in the corridor behind him.

"Lily Petz of Hong Kong," I said, "arranged for me to come here. I'm here to verify that the Ming Dynasty bowls are authentic. I have the purchase money."

"Yes, I know Miss Lily."

His head barely fit within the space between the door and the jamb he had allowed for us to converse.

"Good," I said, growing agitated. "May I come in?"

He swung open the door, took hold of my shoulder and yanked me inside. The door slammed shut, and I followed the lanky torso down an L-shaped foyer. My eyes strained to adjust to the house's dimness, the blacked-out windows and tired bulbs in standing lamps. Sunthorn stopped and gestured at an ornately carved, mother-of-pearl, darkly grained chair. Déjà vu tickled my neck; the chair reminded me of the one in Heifetz's house.

Midnight-blue drapes covered the walls. Boxes, of varying sizes, were piled on top of the long sofa against a far wall. A fluffy blanket with a lion's face had been tossed rather haphazardly over a huge birdcage. Poking its head through the bars, a yellow bird peered at me and chirped. For an instant, I imagined Sunthorn roasting the bird over an outdoor fire. Overhead, the ceiling fixture contained a low-wattage bulb.

"You should have called me," Sunthorn said.

He had about him the stink of a durian.

"I didn't have your number," I replied, sitting down.

A woman emerged from around a corner. She had a pair of red-handled scissors in her right hand. She was a short girl with curly black hair that grazed her shoulder. When she stood beside me, I could see her scalp between the thin black strands. She swung the scissors up to her ear and clicked them once, which emitted the sound of a hissing cat.

"I'd like to check out the Ming bowls," I said.

"What bowls?" the woman said, pointing the scissors at my nose.

I looked at Sunthorn. "What's going on?"

"Who are you?" Sunthorn asked.

"The name is Herman Melville," I said.

Sunthorn lurched in my direction. His hands lifted into half-closed fists, and his shoulders squared with his large womanly hips.

I burst out with a piratical laugh and said, "Hey, big man! Wait a minute!"

"Liar," he mumbled, cocking his right fist.

"Dahling," the woman said to me. "Don't anger him. He has an ulcer."

"Stop!" I shouted.

He wheezed through clenched teeth. "What's your real name?"

"Merlin," I said.

"Merlin! Melville! You weren't sent by Miss Lily! You're here to steal from me!"

He made no move to halt. I rose from the chair and stepped backward only to find my shoulders pressed against the wall. Steadily, Sunthorn approached, his lips sucked in, a drop of spittle on his chin. Quickly the loon was upon me.

His fist shot forward.

The blood spurted from my nose, warm and thick, and I dropped to my knees and pressed my palms into my face. I threw back my head to try to ebb the flow. I coughed, I lurched forward and spat out a glob of mucus and blood. Sitting down on the floor, I pinched my nose with my thumb and forefinger as if the blood would magically clot. I felt light-headed; my stomach heaved. I had swallowed some blood. With my shirttail I tried to stop the bloody outpouring.

I expected a blade next and coughed again. My nose bled copiously, and then I heard the girl say, "Dear, I think he's going to kick you."

I lost whatever courage I had then and puked on the floor.

"Screw the bowls!" I cried out, wiping my mouth with my shirtsleeve. "You can have them!"

"You truly Miss Lily's friend?" Sunthorn asked sheepishly, retreating a few steps from the blood-and phlegm-speckled floor.

"I'm Lily's friend, not a fucking punching bag!"

"He knows Lily," the woman said.

She stood near an open wooden crate, the scissors holstered in her belt.

"Tell me about the bowls," Sunthorn said.

I told him. They were early Ming Dynasty porcelain bowls, decorated in underglaze blue from the reign of Hsuan-tze. "They're bowls from the finest period for blue and white."

I placed a handkerchief to my nose. I could taste the blood in my throat.

"Listen," I said, "forget this bloody nose. I forgive you." Sunthorn grinned for me like a dumb ape. "Yes, I do. I'm big hearted that way. A regular saint I am. Maybe Lily mentioned that. Hit me, steal my money, wreck my car. That's okay. But I'm on a mission for a friend. For Lily. And that's serious. A duty. Now the bowls. Produce them or I might get upset and do something radical," I said, only half joking.

Sunthorn exhaled, and I heard a rattle in his chest. "Over there," he said, jerking his thumb at the opposite wall. "The cardboard box beside the American sign: Budweiser. Your Ming bowls."

I edged by him. The woman followed. Just beyond the window I felt her grab for me, and I jumped, eluding her grasp. Digging into the box, I scooped out balls of Styrofoam, shoveling them onto the floor. Once, for a brief second, I glanced up, sensing a position change on this human game board. The woman had moved to the middle of the room, head lowered, glowering at me. She unnerved me more than Sunthorn. Her gaze appeared as lethal as the scissors in her belt. I didn't like to have my back to her. She had the look of someone who belonged in the bughouse.

I worked quickly. There were three large bowls, and as I deliberately moved the last of the Styrofoam, they appeared, even in the room's shallow light, a worthy treasure. Still, I needed to be sure. I lifted one out of the box. From my shirt pocket, I removed a small magnifying glass and examined the paste, the glaze, and the cobalt oxide painting of the bowl, having originated, supposedly, from the Ming Dynasty. With the boom in Chinese artifacts, fakes, with the tenacity of leeches, had attacked the market. The design was appealing. In the center of the bowl in blue and white, amid a carved-jade pattern, was a boy riding a swan. Next, I ran my finger around the foot of the plate. Through Lily's help, and from years of practical study and experience, I knew the Ming foot tends to be massive and heavy. As I shifted the plate around to verify this fact, the bowl broke in my hand. I ran my finger along the edge. It had been glued. The next bowl fell apart in my hands like a half-baked pie.

"They're broken." In my head, my voice sounded far away. I held the third bowl in my hand. "Why didn't you tell Lily about this?"

Sunthorn said, "I thought she would send a fool. It wasn't my fault. They were damaged in transport."

"Oh Christ," I said.

I let the third bowl fall and shatter on the floor. It was as though I was throwing away everything I had worked for and believed in since my early days in Mexico. I cared little for the money the artifacts might bring me but valued their antiquity and the story held in each porous cell. I pushed the woman out of my way. I hurried away and opened the front door.

"There are other things you can buy," the woman called out.

"Carnivores," I shouted back.

On the street, the evening air was pleasant. Yet, I trembled and sweated as if my body needed to expel the dust and grime that had built up within me from handling legitimate and stolen artifacts for so many years. I suddenly wanted no more contact with such things. I wanted only to be among the living.

When I entered the hotel room I found Melinda in a chair eating a vanilla ice cream cone. She was in her underwear, and her long black hair had been sheared to below her ears.

"What happened to you? You're a bloody mess," Melinda said.

She went into the bathroom, returned with a moist towel and handed it to me. I sat down on the edge of the bed beside her and moved the towel gently around my nose and mouth, wiping away the dried blood. My throat ached, as if my words were suffocating in a water well that had no bottom.

"Sam, what do you think?" Melinda asked. "Do I look like a boy?"

"Exactly."

She shook her head. "It was so hot, so I had my hair cut short. Now my head feels cooler. When we travel I won't be any trouble to you. I'll be strong, and I'll keep up."

I touched her hair. The flat edges tickled my palm. I felt the slim hollow in the back of her neck, so smooth from the blade that had shaved it clean.

"Do you want some ice cream?" she asked.

I shook my head and threw the room key onto the bed. Melinda continued to lick her ice cream cone. "You just missed him, Sam. Wang was here."

I knocked the cone out of her hand, sending it to the floor.

"You saw him like this, in your underwear!"

With her forearm, she wiped a smudge of ice cream from her chin. "Does it matter to you?"

"What are you talking about? It does. It all matters."

She stood, stretched, peeled off her undergarments, and put on her bathrobe.

"Look on the table there," Melinda said.

I went to the nightstand, picked up a black-and-white photograph and held it by its worn edges. There was a man past middle age with graying hair standing beside an Asian woman, short and thin, in an ankle-length dress, who resembled the woman in the photograph I had seen in Hong Kong.

"Wang came here to show me that picture and to try and convince me to go with him. He said he'd pay me. But I told him I wouldn't do it for the money. I told him because the woman in the photo looks so much like me, and that she could be my mother. And only if you go with me." She sat on the bed with her hands inside the big silky pockets. "What do you think? Is this crazy? Will you come?" She hunched forward. "Will you make love with me? Will you do to me what I like so much and place your mouth down here? Why are you so suspicious?"

"I'm jealous," I said.

Somehow, because of Melinda, I had fallen into this foreign realm, and I disliked the way this jealous succubus turned my insides to mush and made me feel like a bumbling idiot.

"I don't care," Melinda said. "I don't want to talk tonight. Now will you calm down? Will you shower? I can't stop asking questions. I want answers for so much. Too much. Like my son. My mother. Where are they? Are they being loved? Do you understand? I want answers, even though I don't have the right questions." She placed her fingers to her chest. "I just want to be taken away for tonight. For a little while. Will you take me away, Sam? I don't want to think tonight. I want you inside me. I want you to hold me. Will you do that? Will you make love to me? Will you come inside me?"

I should have booted her out, but it was more than skin on skin now, or my immersion in her carnal beauty. Melinda was more than a magnificent caryatid whom I would watch when racked with insomnia. It didn't take five years of marriage for her to ravage me. It had taken a month. She had infected my blood, and mental equilibrium, and so I turned almost like an automaton, trying to hold onto the last semblance of my logic.

"Why do you want to go with him?" I asked. "We can be happy here."

She gave me a blasphemous look, disgusted at my sentimentality. She was right. I was concerned solely with myself.

"The money will help me get my son back," Melinda said.

"Some people might say you should never have left him." I hesitated in the wake of her silence. "But it's not the money," I finally said, "is it?"

"No."

"For God's sake, tell me. Why go with him?"

"Mr. Wang knows something about my real mother. Maybe even Jim Thompson does."

"Thompson's dead," I said. "It's all a dodge."

Melinda's robe slithered open, revealing her nakedness, and she quickly covered herself. "A what?" she asked.

"He wants you for himself," I told her.

"Let him think what he wants. It doesn't matter. Even if this is for nothing, I need to take the chance. What can happen?"

I sat in the rooms only chair. "Melinda, the fact is, all along you had your own agenda. You knew Wang was in Bangkok and you never told me. He's your connection to your past. In Hong Kong you thought, *'Why not use this dope Merlin to get to Thailand?'*- That's what was in your head. You kept in touch with Wang through phone calls or letters over the years. I know this. Don't deny it. And then presto! Sam Merlin arrives on the scene and falls for those pretty eyes, and you had your rabbit to Thailand. Yes, and the stories of your dead brother and your son were a smart touch. They added melodrama to the trip. But none of that mattered. I would have taken you with me whether you'd told me the truth or not. I wanted you with me. I fell for you. Of course, how can I ever trust you again?"

"No no no. It was nothing like that. You got it all wrong. Yes, Wang met me at the airport. I planned that. And he told me to meet him at Thompson's house. But I never knew what he wanted. All I wanted was to find out news about my mother. I was going to tell you because you care for me. And I have the same in my heart for you, and more."

Her eyes closed for a moment. She teetered near the brink of exhaustion. The photograph drifted free from my hand.

"Please, pick up the photo. It's a bad omen to leave it on the ground."

"The porcelain bowls are broken," I said.

"They're only objects," Melinda said, very gently.

"No," I said. "They're more. I promised Lily. And now she'll think I've betrayed her."

"I'm sorry. Come to me."

I went toward her and stepped on her ice cream cone, spraying the photograph with a milky film.

"Now you've done it," she said, and crawled beneath the blanket.

After Melinda had fallen asleep, I entered the bathroom, switched on the light, and removed my razor from my toilet kit. It was an old razor my father had given me where the wide, thick bottom unscrews and extra razor blades can be stored inside. I unscrewed it, and out dropped five jewels from the narrow cavern, three rubies and two diamonds. I rubbed them along my palm and marveled at their beauty and value. I knew in that instant they were worth more than the few years' savings I had invested in them. They were Melinda's ticket to her past, and the prize that would not escape me: a life with Melinda. I replaced them in the razor, snapped off the light, and went to bed.

CHAPTER 12

———— ⌘ ————

Two DAYS LATER, Melinda left Bangkok. She took the northeast bound morning train that bore her to Ubon Ratchathani, a town near the Cambodian border where we were to meet Wang and Primo. Wang had reserved the last available ticket. I was able to gain passage through a modest bribe to one of the conductors and ride in a freight car on another train. A local and not an express, the train left Bangkok at six o'clock that evening, scheduled to arrive hours after Melinda's.

In the freight car my companions were five crates of live chickens, bags of rice, suitcases, and a pair of coffins which rested on two two-by-fours. The freight doors were open, and the young Thai boy who managed the compartment sat by himself shuffling through papers as dry, hot gusts swept through the car. I sat on the wooden floor against a wall with my canvas backpack behind me.

Quickly, the sky darkened and the Thai boy turned on two overhead lights. As we approached a low-lying mountain range, the car bounced and one of the coffins shuddered.

"Say, don't those coffins scare you?" I asked the Thai boy.

He lifted his head and smiled. He wore baggy shorts that came down past his knees and a faded purple T-shirt that read *Bob Marley and the Wailers*.

"Who are they?" I asked, gesturing to the coffins.

"I don't know."

The boy spoke English fairly well, for he told me he had been educated at an international high school until his father was killed in a bomb explosion while on business in Narathiwat, a southern province known for Muslim extremists.

"Where are they going?"

"To Surin."

"Hey, I see a fingernail," I said teasingly, gesturing toward one of the coffins.

He came over and sat down next to me. I could feel the smallness of his shoulder and the warmth of his arm against mine.

"Ever hear of *taotaomona*?" he asked me.

I shook my head.

"My mother is from Guam," the Thai boy said, "and that's what my mother's people call spirits. They're shape-shifters. They can change into almost anything--people with fangs, dwarves, different forms of animals. They're evil spirits. They like to shrink children and put them inside co-conut shells where they'll never be found."

His knee touched mine; he was sockless and had slim ankles.

"One evening, when I was a young boy the *taotaomona* woke me from my sleep. My family had just moved into a house that was very old, and the *taotaomona* haunted this house. They came as pigs. They knocked on my window until I got out of bed and then I saw them in the yard, squealing and rolling in the dirt, doing somersaults, waving at me with their tails, wanting me to come and play with them. I saw two climb trees while the other kicked a football. One pig, I remember, smoked a cigarette. I told my family what happened and no one believed me, except my grandmother. She told me to wake her the next time the pigs returned."

He was staring at the dark, wooden rib that bound the coffin shut. "The next night I woke her. She went to the window and saw them in the yard. She told me they were evil, and that they wanted to take my soul. It was a virgin soul they desired. A child's soul. Very precious to them. My grandmother told me that I shouldn't play with them. 'They're the un-happy dead,' she said. 'They might look happy, but they're not.'"

"What did you do?" I asked.

"These were flying pigs!"

"You saw them fly?"

"Yes, and the next night when I went outside to play they said I could fly with them. I was just a boy of eight. I wanted to fly."

"And did you?"

"Of course," he said. "We flew over treetops and circled my mother's garden and my father's half-plowed field. I saw my school and the house where Supot lived, a girl I was fond of. I was suspended by two pigs while the others watched from the ground. But then I saw that the two pigs had wings of bone and tiny baby's hands underneath their bellies. I was frightened and hit one in the snout, and they dropped me. We weren't very high. I ran for my house. My grandmother was at my window, waving for me to come to her, screaming my name. I ran as fast as I could. But they came after me. I heard them laughing and snorting. Soon my grandmother began to throw things at the pigs. She threw a book and my alarm clock. She hit one pig with the clock, and I saw him flip over, but he wasn't dead. He was only playacting. When I made it to my bedroom window my grandmother hauled me inside and slammed the window shut."

He rose awkwardly to his feet. The wind whipped his long black hair, and his shadow filled the rear wall. Beyond the freight doors the sun was down and the land was coal dark. The skinny moon was squeezed behind fleeting clouds. The boy stepped toward the open door, and I wondered if he knew the exact edge of the car.

He turned and raised his hands over his head. A moment later he was dancing, gracefully, similar to the old-style Thai dance.

When the boy put a chicken feather in his hair, I jumped to my feet.

"Do you see pigs?" I asked.

"No," he answered.

"Hallelujah!" I cried.

We did a jig around the coffins. I moved in a shuffle-step, and the boy danced on the balls of his feet, gliding from one end of the car to the other.

Minutes later, tired from the heat and the dance, I leaned against a rice sack. Sitting in his chair, the boy began to sing in a voice so tender I wished to reach out for him, bring him close so I could hear more clearly.

I wanted his hand to touch mine and to place my hand on his shoulder out of a need so simple and elemental it frightened me. I wanted him beside me, this kid who believed in demons and phantoms.

I turned toward the open door, planted my foot against the car's inner wall, and took hold of the door casing. Carefully, I rolled my body around the corner of the door, and with my other hand, grabbed the iron ladder bar outside the car. I opened my mouth, trying to drink the hot breeze. The boy continued to sing, his voice like the restful tintinnabulation of choir bells. I hummed along. Gradually, I leaned farther outside as my body was swept backward by strong blasts of wind. Only my tenuous grip on the wooden casing prevented me from flying out of the car.

I saw the long nose of the train, heard the soft thrum of the engine, and the train wheels gliding over tracks. I released the iron ladder bar. With my hand held out, zephyr-like blasts hit my palm, and when I flattened my hand, I rode the currents like a glider, giving way to the bumps and grinds of tiny air pockets. Ever so slightly, the train turned, moving my body away from the car, drawing me outside. The engine whistle wailed, and the train arced, following a curve in the track.

Mysteriously, the Thai boy had stopped singing. The passenger lights in the train windows were extinguished, and the ground swept by in a blur, our speed impossible to calculate. For a moment I was tempted to bend low, touch the ground with my foot.

"Hey!" I heard the boy shout. "Look!"

With great effort, I pulled myself inside the car. The boy stood pointing at the rear of the compartment. One of the coffins was moving, sliding forward off its two-by-four support. The other coffin had a slight wobble to it.

The Thai boy hurried forward and stood near me, with the open door between us. The coffin that had begun to slide bolted off the two-by-four onto the floor and shivered briefly from side to side as it crept toward us. The train continued to climb around the mountain, our car at a twenty-degree tilt, and I could hear the train's engine grinding under the strain. The bags of rice shifted and a suitcase broke loose from its binding. Its latches snapped, and the case sprung open revealing lacy underclothing, hair brushes, a photograph of Naowarat, the Thai matinee idol, and came to rest against a mountainous rice bag. Beneath my feet, the wooden floor vibrated.

The train slowed further. As the upgrade intensified, the coffin slithered ahead, halted as it hit a knot in the wooden floor, rose once from a jarring vibration and skidded out the door. We watched it whip by us, amazed at its sudden velocity. I gazed outside. For an instant, the coffin hung suspended in the air but soon fell, the cheap wood splintering apart, appearing to disintegrate as it rolled across the ground, the sound like the final moan of a burning house. On the small slope of dirt and rock graded away from the track, the small body rose into a sitting position. Within moments, I lost sight of the grandmother.

When I turned fully around, the other coffin had toppled its two-by-four support. It landed on the floor at a forty-five degree angle, with the front end pointed in my direction. The coffin moved across the rough-hewn floor, skittering back and forth as the train, in a lower speed, climbed at an even steeper grade. As the coffin wiggled its way forward, I feared it wouldn't make it through the door. I envisioned the scene, the coffin's lid and sides splitting apart, the body popping through the paltry wood, a foot kicking its way free, next the fingers, wrist and arm. Like Lazarus it would rise, clad in its finest clothes, pushing through the wood, and thanking us with a wolfish grin.

When the coffin was within inches of my feet, I reached out with both hands and took hold of the lid. I held the coffin in place, hindering its progress. But the momentum behind the coffin increased.

As the pressure intensified against my hand, the train gave a mighty shake, and our car shifted dramatically from left to right, sending the coffin spinning. The coffin's rear end hit the wall where the Thai boy stood on the other side of the door. Particles of wood flew across the car, and several nails shot loose. The rear of the coffin caved in. Then the train jolted and a foot flopped through the broken section of the coffin.

The foot, encased in a red leather slipper, trembled from the car's motion. A brown stocking covered the upper arch. Abruptly the car slanted again, and the coffin, trapped between the Thai boy and me, rotated and slammed into my side of the open door. The sound was dull, and the coffin seemed unaffected. A minute later the rear of the coffin collapsed, and both legs of the occupant, past the calves, were exposed.

"We should do something!" the Thai boy shouted.

"Yes," I agreed. "We should jump."

"Impossible," the boy replied.

I shrugged, kicking pieces of wood out the door. The body seemed to resist its easy access through the open door, toward a more welcome world. I tapped the upper intact portion of the coffin near the occupant's shoulder and head. The Thai boy walked over and pulled away chunks of the ruined coffin, wood that came off easily in his hand. He went to work: he tore off the lid and chucked it outside, kicked down the side closest to him and hauled the body out.

The ringless hands rested across the small bosom. He sat the body up. It took some doing. Her joints were pretty useless. Both the interior casket and the body had been salted with a perfume solution that masked the ghastly smell. Her legs were pointed at the black landscape. The red slipper tassels leaped in the wind. The boy studied the slight figure and the painted face. With a solid push between the shoulder blades, the Thai boy delivered the woman past the car door and into the night.

"Why did you do that?" I asked him, as he stood motionless, panting.

"She didn't belong here," he said.

"Didn't belong?"

"I didn't want her here as if she were alive."

He sat on the floor, in the open doorway, his legs dangling over the edge. He seemed composed. One of the coffin nails rolled against his thigh, and he placed it in his pocket.

We were traveling only a few miles per hour. The boy's hands gripped the end of the wooden plank. His back was very straight, his face alert and peaceful. I cannot recall ever seeing a more beautiful face on a boy.

"I wonder who she was," I said.

"My grandmother," he answered. "I was taking her to Surin for cremation."

I glanced outside, expecting something. Perhaps an acknowledgement of a good deed, or a cry of dissolution. For now, without cremation, the grandmother's spirit would be bound to this earth. Still, if the truth be known, I was glad she was gone, even though it appeared we had abandoned her.

The boy stared at the dark ground that swept blindly beneath his feet. Elbows bent, his hands tightly held onto the floor's edge.

"What are you doing?" I asked.

"I have to protect her," he said. "There are snakes and mad dogs in the mountains. She's old, but I'm sure they'll find her tasty. There's also the *taotaomona*. They'll steal her body and bargain god for her soul. They're heartless, those demons." He sighed. "I'll bury her so she'll be safe."

Before I could utter a plea, he jumped out of the car. I poked my head beyond the doors. He rolled along the ground and quickly regained his footing. He didn't wave. Even when I shouted, he refused to answer. I watched his body recede, a tiny relief sculpture shrinking and disappearing against a larger landscape. When I turned around the car seemed huge and unfriendly. Strips of wood were scattered about the compartment. Coffin nails rattled along the floor. I leaned against the wall for a moment, turned, and leaped into the darkness.

It didn't take long to find him. Fortunately, the moon was out as I followed the railway ties. He was digging at the ground with a stick and not making much headway. The action was more a pawing motion. It was a happy night, all right. I found another stick and worked beside him, stabbing at the dirt, brushing away handfuls onto a small but growing mound.

His grandmother lay a few feet away, staring right at us. He had rolled her onto her side. Her shoes were gone, her clothes untidy, and in the moonlight her mouth was curled downward, as if the tumble off the train car had caused her some discomfort. She moved my soul in an awkward and disturbing manner. Even with the death of Kamaldeep in Kabul, I hadn't felt so violated by the dead. It was as though I were to blame for her burial in this empty region.

We didn't pause. We both wanted to finish this ceremony. When my stick broke, I used the heels of my shoes and kicked at the dirt. The deeper we went the earth seemed to relent, losing its toughness. There is a holiness to the act of burial, or so I have read and seen in movies. But it's not true. The only holiness is in living. So, when we lifted his grandmother and placed her into the hole, neither of us spoke. We just pushed the dirt pile over her.

If there were animals nearby eventually they would find her. We had not buried her very deep. I felt bad about this and knew my presence had only speeded up the digging that deserved a more caring and deliberate process. The boy shivered as we stood next to his buried grandmother. Had I the power to resurrect her, I would have for the boy's sake. But such thoughts are fairytales, even though the dead have spoken and material- ized before me in disquiet moments.

"We should push on," I said.

I walked a few meters away to give the boy time alone with his grand- mother. But within moments he appeared beside me waiting, it seemed, for a signal of some kind. None appeared. The living often search for heav- enly signs in the most unlikely and ridiculous places. Years ago, I would often pass the same stumblebum in the same New York City alley on the way to my office. Sometimes, I would drop a few bills into his plastic cup. Often, I would see him pacing in the alley, as if in search of his wallet. If there is one place where god should appear, it was in that alley, for the lost are the most in need.

Just after dawn we walked into Surin station. The sun cowered behind a pink sky, and a few people milled about on the train platform. Cocks, imprisoned in cages near the platform, cackled in the crisp, morning air. Seated on benches, sleepy-eyed women waited for the train with baskets of food at their feet. The air hung thick with barbecued skewered meat that smelled heavenly, steamed rice, pale brown-sugar cookies, colorful fruit drinks in plastic bags, the pungent smell of charcoal fires, and manure from the nearby fields. Flies buzzed the food in an aerial dogfight.

"Thank you," the boy said.

I gave him some money. The boy *wai*-ed and walked toward town. Another train would arrive in a few hours. Just beyond the station platform, bicycle samlors waited in a barren yard for a passenger. I sat beside one of the women on the bench, bought several small oranges from her, and ate them in the shade of the station building.

I found Melinda at the Regent Palace pool enjoying the accommodations she had arranged for us before we left Bangkok. She lay on a lounge chair beneath a striped beach umbrella. Her slender body, slick from a recent swim, was covered in a single-piece black bathing suit. A towel covered her ankles. She was reading a book I would soon know well, as dear to her as her prayers, *The Life of Buddha* by Asvaghosa.

She took off her sunglasses. "I was worried about you."

"What room are we in?"

"Twenty-three."

She removed the key that she had been using as a bookmark from between two pages and handed it to me.

"I'm going inside," I said.

I entered the room, removed my shoes and socks, and lay down in my clothes on the soft mattress, disturbing the white sheets. The room's bluish-green walls and carpet made me feel as though I were submerged below a calm sea. I could hear a slight drip from the bathroom faucet.

When Melinda came in minutes later she stood off to the side, near the opposite wall, and said in a flat tone, "What took you so long? You're a day late."

I couldn't talk to her; I was exhausted. Instead, I waved in a feeble response for her to come closer. I wanted to speak to her of mundane matters like my growing love for her, and the colorful Scarlet Minivet bird that trilled near our window. *I love you*, I wanted to say. It seemed like such a simple thing to express.

"I thought you were going to desert me. Was that your plan? Were you going to leave me without a word, Sam?"

I shook my head.

"I drank brandy last night. It tasted like licorice. And I drank until I was drunk, or thought I was drunk, and then I got scared."

"Why scared?"

"I didn't know where I was going to sleep. I couldn't find my money. It seemed like a big deal, having a place to sleep." She studied my face. "You're dirty," she said, and went into the bathroom and wet a towel.

Sitting beside me on the mattress, she unbuttoned my shirt and removed it. She sponged my face, chest, arms, and hands. When she was through I held up my hand, shading my eyes from the sunlight that rolled in through the window, so I could see her more clearly. She looked away and closed the thin curtains. The room barely darkened. Without a word, she kicked off her sandals, removed her bathing suit, and reached for her book. She peeled back the white bed sheet and stretched out beside me, her body sweet smelling from tanning lotion and chlorine, her book opened and held to her chest. I remember falling asleep to something familiar and pleasant, and even today can recall Melinda reading, and the soothing sound of pages being turned in her old book.

CHAPTER 13

A DEEP BLUE edged the early morning sky, and the penumbra of the moon was still visible in the western quadrant. Melinda and I sat on a wooden bench in the rear of the truck with Wang and Primo across from us. A cold wind whistled and snapped the canvas flaps. Out of the city, we passed an ancient foreign-made car, a horse-drawn cart of vegetables and fruits, and a truck crammed with swine. After a brief stop at a rest area, where we refueled and bought bottled water, the truck rolled into the mountains.

"We'll ride for a few hours," Wang said. "After we eat, we'll start walking. It'll be at least a three-day hike, maybe more, before we reach the village and Thompson."

The trek began at noon. Tee-Wah, our guide, a short, dark-skinned Thai with a boyish, handsome face, took point. At first, the dirt trail was smooth and flat, wide enough so Melinda and I walked side by side. By mid-afternoon the trail narrowed and rose abruptly toward a peaked mountain range. Soon our boots were thickly dusted from the red soil. The higher we climbed, the denser the vegetation became, taking on varied shades of green.

As we marched onward, winding higher along the mountain, the narrow trail changed into a ledge and our footing grew treacherous, the ground pitted with small, sharp boulders. Like wild weeds, the vegetation and forest sprang up at us from the land below.

After hours of walking, we rested before a two-hundred-foot waterfall. There were no bird calls or animal groans. The only sound was the splashing falls.

"There are bandits," Wang said, seated beside me.

Somehow he had finagled his way between Melinda and me.

"It's because of the Golden Triangle, the poppy fields," Primo said, dousing his head with water.

Wang touched Melinda's knee. "Are you scared, my dear?"

"Of what?"

"The bandits. Well, don't be. We're only skirting their territory."

I knocked him in the thigh with my fist and he lifted his hand from Melinda's knee. "What's the name of the village we're going to?" I asked.

"It's near Preah Vihear," answered Wang. "It was the site of a minor disaster. During the Cambodian famine of the 1970s, Thai soldiers had killed 45,000 Cambodian peasants by shoving them off the Preah Vihear cliffs. Thousands died from land mines that lined the paths or were shot by Thai soldiers if they tried to return. We'll have to be careful. There are still live landmines."

Tee-wah, who sat away from the group, said, "I told you I won't take you into Cambodia."

"I know," Wang said curtly. "I'm not asking you to."

"It's not a good idea for you to go, either," Tee-wah said to Melinda. "The Khmer Rouge are still here, hidden in secret groups in dangerous cells."

Wang laced his fingers below his chin and said, "Buddha will protect us."

"Look!" I half shouted, springing to my feet.

A wild boar no more than twenty-five yards in front of us raced through the undergrowth. Seconds later a menacing tiger loped after the boar. Everyone stood and hastened forward to the trail's edge. Bushes and palm leaves shook. The boar snorted, and a flash of striped fur followed in pursuit.

"Where are they?" Melinda asked.

Tee-wah stepped up next to her. "To your left. They're moving away. But the tiger was up here." He pointed at the soft dirt. "Pug marks. Tracks left by the tiger's feet."

"What's going to happen?" she asked him.

"Most likely the tiger will kill the boar. Unless it's a weretiger."

"What's that?" she asked.

"It's a man who can turn into a tiger and changes back before he kills." He got down on one knee and examined the track. "A tiger has four toes. All cats have four toes. But a weretiger has five toes. This beast has five toes."

"There's no such thing," I said.

"Sam, look! It does have five toes," Melinda said, staring at the faint impression.

Wang tugged on my sleeve. "A tiger trophy would please Jim Thompson. I have a pistol you could use."

I suddenly recalled seeing bodies stacked like cords of wood in Afghanistan during the Afghan-Soviet War, where I had gone in search of the ancient doll.

"Don't shoot him," Melinda said.

I turned and, for a split second, in the dazzling sunlight, Melinda and Tee-wah looked to be husband and wife, his short, thin reedy frame beside her delicate torso, his hairless arms and chest a shade darker than hers.

"We should go," Tee-wah said.

"Yes, we're jerks just staying here," said Primo, moving up the trail.

We walked in single file. An hour later I caught a distinctive, nauseating smell in the still air. I was about to speak when Wang said, "That's opium."

We continued down the trail, snaking deeper into the jungle until we reached several blankets hanging on a line. A man sat outside the blankets, a rifle across his lap, the muzzle pointing at us. Tee-wah spoke hoarsely, "Don't look and don't say a word."

We walked onward. When we had traversed some three hundred yards and were out of sight, Tee-wah said, "They're smugglers taking an opium smoke break behind the blankets. The man with the gun was the sentry. If he thought we were the police or other smugglers, we'd be dead."

"Thank you," Melinda said, reaching out and placing her hand on Tee-wah's shoulder. "We're lucky you're here."

An hour later, lounging beneath a palm tree, a boy hailed Tee-wah. They wai-ed one another. His name was Chow, but Tee-wah said we should call him Joe. Joe smiled. His teeth were stained crimson; he had been chewing betel nut, a juicy nut that gives one a mild high. Joe joined Tee-wah in front of the line and guided us until dusk.

As we entered the Palong village, children ran down the dirt road, stopped, and stared at us. In the long shadow of their huts, women, clothed in bright reds and blues, in long-sleeved blouses and ankle-length skirts, threshed rice in large bowls with a wooden mallet. The village had no electricity, only kerosene lanterns which, one by one, twinkled on as daylight faded.

We dumped our gear in a roomy hut, made up of straw mats, which would be our sleeping quarters for the night.

Wang and Primo went out, talking in whispers. Tee-wah and Joe disappeared into another hut with one of the tribesmen.

In the last glimmer of twilight, a group of children stood huddled in the hut's opening. Melinda waved them in and distributed a pen to each child. She had stowed a couple of dozen pens in her backpack, knowing they were precious items and represented tribal authority.

"Are you glad you came?" I asked her, noticing her joy as she handed out the pens.

"Yes, very. And you?"

"Me too."

A small boy, confused by the object, held his pen out to Melinda. She took it, removed the cap, and drew several lines with the ballpoint on the palm of her hand. The children, who had retreated after receiving their gift, moved closer and surrounded Melinda. She opened her other hand and one by one allowed each child to make a mark. They drew squiggly lines, circles, dots, and one child penned a nose on Melinda's palm. They laughed, thrilled by their new gift, and pressed their fingers against the blue ink markings and then drew on their own hands.

"I should have brought paper," Melinda said, as she helped a willowy girl press down on her Bic pen, revealing the ballpoint. "This way they could see the real magic of a pen."

I laughed. "A pen? Magical?"

"Yes. You don't think so?"

She was quite serious. Her eyes and fingers shifted from child to child as they remained close to her, experimenting with their new toy. From her knapsack she tore out paper from a journal, something I had never seen before or knew she kept.

"You write letters, don't you?" she asked in a most pleasant voice so as not to send the children scurrying. "I write to my son. That's magic. The same as the childhood dreams you told me about at the orphanage. My son can read the things in my heart, or the person reading my letters can read them to him."

"Do you think she reads your letters to your son?"

Melinda distributed the sheets of paper, but the children only stuffed them down their trousers. They enjoyed writing on their hands. A few sat on the dirt floor having kicked off their flimsy sandals and had begun to draw on their ankles. Melinda took the youngest girl by the waist and drew her against her body. She didn't struggle. Melinda had given her the only red ink pen.

"I don't know. I can only hope she reads my letters to him."

The possibility that she would ever see her son again seemed remote. The child in her arms was so alive, and the sadness of this deception was a world removed. But the tragedy, of course, the treachery we are blind to, was that she believed, like so many, her dream would come true.

CHAPTER 14

IN THE EVENING, we sat on the floor in the chief tribesman hut, with four hefty plates of food in front of us. It was our first meal of the day. There was meat, vegetables, and noodles cooked with curry, lemongrass, ginger, and spices, all of which I devoured, being famished, and found delicious. Wood smoke clogged my nostrils and burned my eyes. Still, I kept eating, out-dueling Primo for seconds and thirds, sweating, and gulping water. I removed my sweater at one point. Outside, the temperature had dropped since the sun had fallen, but the cramped hut was warm, lit by kerosene lanterns. Pushing aside my wooden spoon, I ate with my fingers, swallowing, slurping on a piece of curried roasted meat, feeding Melinda a spicy noodle I wrapped around my fork, so she had to untwine it with her fingers.

The dishes and plates lay empty, tilted, overturned, juices streaking their sides. Melinda yawned, and I removed a stringy piece of meat from her chin. Her head rested against my shoulder. She patted her stomach and belched. I loved her appetite. She devoured each course with the same relish, though she never gained an ounce.

"You ate a lot," I said.

"It's my heart," she explained, stroking her belly, her belt buckle loosened. "My heart beats twice as fast as ordinary people. A sign of Queens, I read in a magazine. It also makes me a great lover."

We stacked our plates, and the chief's wife carted the dishes into the tiny galley. A few feet from the eating area, Tee-wah played checkers by candlelight with the chief, who, with grubby fingers, appeared to cheat when Tee-wah turned his head to look at his attractive wife. The game, played on a cardboard square with bottle caps for pieces, was the center of activity. At one point the chief's wife hunched over her husband's shoulder and clucked her tongue, disagreeing with his last move.

During the meal, I had noticed several pens clipped to the chief's shirt, a sign of his power and influence.

A few minutes after Wang and Primo departed, Melinda and I left the chief's hut. Inside our hut, Melinda scooted onto our straw mat, shivering beneath two heavy blankets. A lit kerosene lamp burned. With her head exposed, she blew a frosty breath at me and peeled away the thick layers, invitingly. I knelt down, pulled up her heavy shirt, and kissed her belly. She placed her fingers in my hair. I lifted her bra and kissed her breasts. I was beyond infatuation or lust, beyond love. With a light touch of her hand, she moved me away from her breasts and kissed my mouth. We heard voices approaching, most likely Wang and Primo. As they approached, I sat up and told her I was going to the nearby stream to wash and would return shortly. Her breathing was deep. She was near exhaustion after the long march and feast and kissed me, her tongue brushing my lips.

"Why are you leaving me?" she asked in a tender voice.

"I can't sleep. The walk will do me good."

"What are you afraid of?"

I couldn't tell her. I dare not. For who truly believes in ghosts nowadays, and who believes that one's actions or gestures as a young man can haunt one so many years later?

Wang and Primo entered the hut.

As I left, Wang said, "It doesn't get much better than this, does it, Merlin?"

"I'll wait for you," Melinda called out.

I carried a bar of soap and a towel. Earlier in the evening, during twilight, I had watched a woman washing her clothes by the riverbank, whipping the wet shirt she had just dunked in the stream against a boulder, as two boys hunted for fish and splashed each other.

Sweeping the flashlight's beam across the sloping ground, I walked cautiously. I could see only the earth that the light illuminated.

I heard the stream first, like a giggle, and saw its reflected surface in the crescent moonlight. On the bank, I stepped out of my boots and socks and rolled up my pant legs. The night was cloudless and cool, and the stars arced radiantly in the pure black sky. I laid my flashlight against a log, walked into the flowing murmur and positioned myself midway in the stream. Against my ankles the stream ran strong and cold, the footing treacherous. At first I played a game, shifting my weight from one leg to the other, hopping on each foot, testing my balance. As I lowered my cupped hands to the surface, my foot slipped on the slick riverbed stones, and I tumbled backward into the water. I howled. My hands flopped in the teeth-chilling current, and the water beat against my chest. I felt the current push against my belly, trying to ease me downstream. My pants were soaked and my testicles ached.

In the mishap, I lost my soap and towel. I slapped at the water and struggled out of the stream. Upon reaching land, I wrapped my arms across my chest and realized I stood on the other side of the river, away from the village and my flashlight.

Behind me the woods fanned out against the darkness. Shivering, I stepped away from the stream toward the woods. As though touched by an illusionist, I saw the Afghan corpses of men, women, and children. They lay against the tree trunks, piled up to the branches.

"I'm sorry," I said, and instantly regretted it.

I had done nothing wrong. In early 1988, at Salang Afghanistan, in search of a rare relic, --a pair of pendants known as the "Dragon Master" and stolen from the Tillya Tepe tombs-- I had been a terrified witness to the Soviet military slaughter in this village. People were taken out of their houses, cars, mosques, and shops by Russian soldiers, then. Lined up and shot. The shooting went on from morning to night.

Turning, I stumbled forward and waded across the stream, slipping twice on the stones. Crawling onto the bank, I sat against a boulder. My knee hurt, and blood dripped along my shin.

"A late-night swim?" a voice said from the blackness.

I squinted. "Who's there?"

"I hope you aren't seriously injured."

Footsteps neared, and Wang came into view carry a flashlight. "You must be cold," he said.

He pressed the tip of his shoe against my injured knee. I sprang away from him and knocked my head against the boulder.

"Yes, just as I thought. You're bleeding." He threw down a shirt. "Put this on. You'll catch your death in these mountains. And it's not your time to die, now is it? A young man like yourself."

I stood and stripped off my drenched shirt, pants, and underwear. Already a chill ripped through my skin, attacking my bones. Naked and flinging my wet clothes onto the ground, Wang stared at me as if I were a circus clown. His shirt was made of thick flannel, warm to the skin. He must have had it draped over the sweater he wore.

"What are you doing down here?" I asked. "Just strolling?"

"I couldn't sleep. It's a problem of mine."

It irritated me that we had something in common.

"That's too bad," I said. "I always sleep like a log."

"You're fortunate."

He lit a fresh cigarette with the one dangling from his lips, which was smoked down to its nub, then flicked the spent butt away.

"I'm glad I've stumbled upon you," he said, blowing a wreath of smoke up at the moon. "I've been meaning to speak with you about Melinda. I'm going to need your help, good fellow. There's something in this expedition for you. I gathered you figured that out. Otherwise you wouldn't have come. How does gold sound to your greedy ear?"

"I'm not interested in that," I said.

"Silence. I'll be quick."

I sat at his feet, putting on my socks and boots. It angered me that he stood so close, as his pudgy face peered down at me. I swept the shirttail over my privates. A red ember spiraled down close to my leg. With his boot toe, Wang snubbed out the glowing cigarette, as if he were crunching a small human bone. He resumed speaking when I stood. He was a polite Chinese gent.

"Thompson has gobs of money," Wang said. "And sheets of gold. They're both tucked away somewhere. How do you think he survived the Khmer Rouge all these years? On his good looks? He's old, consumptive, blind in one eye, has gall stones, croons like a loon when he shits. I'm a bit poetic tonight." He reached into his pants' pocket and pulled out a pint bottle of whiskey. "For you, sir?"

I waved him off. He took a sip and dropped it back in his pocket.

"If Thompson likes Melinda and thinks she's his daughter, he'll tell her where his fortune is hidden. He could even rewrite his will and explain to the world he's alive. With a little luck, he'll leave his house and his business to us, his new heirs. I've been like a son to him for years."

"And what do you want from me?"

"Coax Melinda. Allow her to feed on Thompson's sympathy. She really does look like his dead wife. He's old and a fool at times. His hands shake, his eyes droop. I believe he wears diapers. He's incontinent like an old horse. A little push in the right direction and we're rich."

I yanked on the shirt. My lower extremities were riddled with goose flesh. An owl hooted in the forest behind us, and my body trembled.

"It's only an owl," Wang said. "They're good luck charms to these hill people."

The Afghans weren't there, but I could smell the corpses ripening like week-old fruit beneath the branches, even in this weather. It may have been a pile of dung or a dead animal but the fear was real. Nonetheless, I knew if I was to survive I had to torch the Afghan dead from my memory. Looking up the hill, I had the sudden desire to run back to Melinda. The taste of her mouth and body would see me through the night, quiet these wraiths who beckoned me from the darkness.

"So you'll help me," Wang said.

"No way."

"Where we're going the Khmer don't like strangers, especially Westerners."

"Good."

"Don't pretend you're brave," he said.

I picked up my soggy clothing. The owl perched on a nearby rock.

"I didn't think we were going into Cambodia," I said, feeling the weight of the wet clothes on my arm.

"We're not. But the border is close."

"Tell me one thing. Is that woman in the photograph related to Melinda?"

"Of course," said Wang. "That's the truth. Merlin, I'll be counting on your cooperation. It'll be helpful for everyone's safety."

For some reason, I was glad for the lie and the veiled threat. This made my appearance seem functional, a part of the plan.

Wang departed, heading downstream. The flashlight beam bounced along the ground and shortly disappeared.

I grabbed my glowing flashlight and hiked up the hill. Before I entered the hut, I snapped off the flashlight. Inside, like a child cowering in the dark, I placed my hand on my heart. I was afraid. It was as though something had separated from within me, and no matter how I struggled to suppress it, keep it down, it struggled upward through my arteries and skin. I felt it slip out of me, my soul, perhaps, searching for a home, or a compatriot in this comic universe. Then, from the corner mat, Melinda whispered my name.

CHAPTER 15

THE NEXT MORNING I climbed onto an elephant with the aid of a ladder and platform, expecting Melinda to follow.

Tee-wah stroked my elephant's flank. "Melinda can't ride with you," he called up at me.

I looked down. "Why not?" I asked, patting the elephant's crown.

The elephant's skin was rough as sandpaper with several black hairs a foot long, coarse as a wire brush.

"The people in this village believe in Spirits. It's their religion. Animism. Your elephant is male, and a woman can't ride a male elephant. The Spirits won't like it. It's bad luck," he said calmly, leading my elephant away from the platform. "You'll ride alone."

A few yards away Tee-wah climbed onto his elephant, a female I was certain, as Melinda hopped up behind him, and dropped her hands onto Tee-wah's hips.

As we exited the village, the children and many of the women waved farewell. We rode in single file. Tee-wah and Melinda took front position. Primo and Wang brought up the rear. Soon we dropped off the dirt road onto a ragged path. The mild air gradually grew heavy and damp as we tramped beneath a canopy of leafy trees. Joe, with a long stick in his hand, walked behind Primo and Wang's elephant, whipping the stick across the animal's hind legs. Every time the stick struck, their elephant quickened and nudged mine with its trunk.

I could hear Joe laughing, probably buzzed from the betel nut he chewed.

"Pick up the pace!" Primo shouted.

I turned and raised my fist as Joe's lash swept across the elephant's rump. Expressionless, their animal galloped forward and bumped my elephant, which moved us at an odd angle with the path.

"Pull its ears!" Joe yelled to me. "She'll obey!"

"Okay!"

Taking hold of one enormous ear, I tugged fiercely. My elephant remained unimpressed. In fact, he seemed to slow down, bemused, it appeared, by my tender gesture. My rump bounced on the rope saddle, and my legs dangled useless on either side of his torso. Desperate, I seized his ear again and yanked with such force that this time we bolted forward, galloping at an alarming pace, trampling dried scrub brush that edged the path. The initial lurch had bounced me to the front of the saddle, and I dug my knees into his neck and took hold of the sparse, tough hair on his head for balance. His huge feet stepped clumsily over small boulders. We traveled on the path's rim, skirting the forest to our left that dropped precariously. Beneath me, I felt the animal's shifting weight, the huge muscles, and smelled the scented soap that had been used to wash him before we left the Palong village but could not quite mask his rank odor. His breathing was labored. He was an aged beast.

We lumbered up alongside Tee-wah and Melinda. I yelled at them as we rumbled past, "You could build a fence around that brute!"

"Slow down, Sam!" Melinda yelled. "You'll break your neck!"

We took the lead as the path grew more treacherous with larger stones and a thickening jungle. My elephant instinctively seemed to know his way. Through the palm fronds overhead, glimpses of blue sky appeared. We passed basil, coffee, pepper, and white poppy fields. Five minutes later, our pace decreased. Tipsy from exhaustion, the elephant drifted from one side of the path to the other. Soon the oppressive heat of the day slowed us to a crawl, and we returned to our original formation, second in line behind Tee-wah and Melinda. Joe, weary of walking, rode with me.

For the rest of the journey the group traveled in silence, muted by the heat, as our elephants doggedly pressed onward. Hours later, Melinda placed her head between Tee-wah's shoulderblades. Her back heaved as she took deep breaths, fatigued by the arduous ride. I wanted to say something, but I remained silent as she drifted off to sleep, her head limp against Tee-wah's back, her cheek pressed to his sweaty shirt.

At one point, he reached behind her and placed his hand against her lower spine. She awoke briefly, draped her hands on his shoulders and moved her lips to his ear. What did she say to him? The words, I imagined, had nothing to do with me, and were spoken in a language I was not privileged to know. She was drawn to him, and when we finally arrived at camp, they had to separate themselves like lovers, peeling slowly away from one another's sweat-stained bodies.

CHAPTER 16

IT WAS A small camp of many huts in a dry plain surrounded by the Dangrek Mountains. But this time, unlike the Palong village, no one came out to welcome us. The camp appeared deserted, except for several half-starved dogs lying belly-down in the brown dust.

Joe took the elephants behind a wooden shelter on our left to be fed, and Tee-wah disappeared into one of the huts. The four of us sat in the shade beneath a tree.

Finally, Wang remarked, "Up there. Straight ahead. Just over the hill and down the cliff. That's where Thompson lives. No more than a one-day walk."

"Yeah," said Primo, putting his feet up on his big pack. "That's fucking Cambodia."

"You mean Thompson lives in Cambodia?"

"Did I forget to mention that?" Wang said. "Oh, forgive me."

In the day's light, I noted the land bridge, a steep dirt path down a mountainside that linked Thailand with Cambodia.

Within minutes, Melinda fell asleep with her head in my lap. Primo, as well, had dozed off. Later, I watched two men enter the village. One hauled a bunch of coconuts in his *kramar*, and the other carried rice in a pouch slung over his shoulder. They took no notice of us, and when they passed an old woman threshing rice, they handed her one of the smaller coconuts in exchange for some tobacco or marijuana.

Somehow, Joe returned by the Cambodian land bridge between the mountains. He must have worked his way to the Cambodian side by a secret route. He looked sullen and called for Tee-wah, who emerged from the hut smoking a cheroot.

They sat off by themselves, crouched beside the hut, discussing earnestly the news Joe had brought.

"When do we see Thompson?" I asked Wang.

"Depends on what Joe knows. We're at the mercy of the Khmer now."

I turned my head. Wang sat behind me. He lifted his ball cap that had been drawn over his eyes.

"The Khmer Rouge? I thought you were kidding."

"The Khmer are merciless," Wang said. "They kill indiscriminately. There's always some group in need of extinction. That's what history teaches us, doesn't it? So, in order to survive, Merlin, we turn a half-blind eye, grab the loot, and enjoy life."

He pulled the cap down. It was too hot to talk.

I was sure, though, he meant to use the word *extermination*. But either way, the more I sat in the breezeless shade contemplating the sorry-ass bridge between these two nations, the stronger the awareness of my mistake became: I should never have come along. My actions, even my thoughts, I felt, were precipitating some disaster, one I couldn't yet fathom.

Melinda twisted in my lap. Her mouth left a wet spot on my pants leg. She slept and sweated as if consumed in a febrile memory. I tried to comfort her. With my handkerchief, I wiped perspiration from her brow.

At first, they appeared as dark spots against a harsh sky, making their way antlike across the bridge. A couple of them held hands and sang, lowly, in pleasant voices. Their trousers were rolled up to the knee. They neared, nonchalantly, out of ranks. Their clothes and faces looked scrubbed clean, and their height was no more than five-foot-five inches tall. Several of the group of ten smiled in a demented way that made me uneasy. The only things that separated them from the older children in Palong, beside their so-called smiles, were the weapons strapped to their backs and the bandoleers of ammunition across their chests.

The singing stopped, and I felt an instant tightening in my groin. At that moment, Melinda sat up and rubbed her eyes. For days, before

Melinda and I left Bangkok, I had fortified my knowledge of Cambodia with books, interviews, and television documentaries on the suspicion that we might venture near the Cambodian border. I wanted to prepare myself for the unexpected.

If they were not Khmer Rouge, they may have been the Khmer Sereikar who were known to have run the bloodthirsty Khmer Rouge from power and been ousted themselves by the Vietnamese in 1979. In 1991 the Vietnamese withdrew from Cambodia, and a transitional government run by King Norodom Sihanouk, the Khmer Rouge opposition, was established. His monarchy dated to the ancient Khmers of twelfth-century Angkor. These days, Hun Sen, a former Khmer Rouge agent, and his government cronies, ran the country and had for decades.

When they got within a few meters the soldiers unshouldered their weapons and pointed the muzzles at us. They didn't direct us to any particular spot, shoo us to the bridge or back into the forest where we had come from. They seemed pleased just to train their weapons on us. It gave them something to do. They were a merry band.

Three wore scarves full of Buddhist charms. Many had their shirts unbuttoned and showed off tattoos. The scarves were inscribed with spells, and the tattoos, thought to be powerful magic, were to protect them from enemy bullets. The mercenary group also wore sunglasses, and one boy had a bayonet tucked inside his boot. The leader, a plump boy of about fifteen who held his pistol on us, a .45 caliber, smoked a black cigarette, a recent product called Death I had seen on Thai store shelves.

Tee-wah went over and spoke to them. When they stopped talking, Tee-wah said to us, "I think they want money."

"You think?" I asked.

"I don't understand the Khmer language so well."

The leader said something to his band, and they talked among themselves. A few laughed. They were a chatty bunch. The leader spoke to Tee-wah again, wagging his pistol at our faces.

"Baht or dollars," exclaimed Tee-wah in a firmer voice. "He wants money."

"We want to see Thompson first," said Wang. "Tell him--"

Before Wang could finish the leader spoke again, his voice pitched higher.

Tee-wah turned toward us. "He remembers you, Mr. Wang. He says you stole money from his brother-in-law in a gambling game. Is that true?"

"Tell that hooligan it was an honest game. A simple game of chance."

Tee-wah looked uncomfortable. "Please. Give him what money you have."

I reached into my pocket and handed Tee-wah Thai baht notes. From my travels, I had learned it was wise to keep dollars and Thai baht in several locations. Robbery and extortion were always possible, so handing over the Thai baht was not a problem. I also wished to keep Melinda safe. Tee-wah took the notes and gave it over to the chubby boy.

The leader talked, and Tee-wah said, "He's happy. Thank you Mr. Sam for your generosity."

They withdrew, slinging their weapons on their shoulders.

"I thought this was Thai soil," I said, watching them near the bridge. "How can the Khmer Rouge come and go like that? Aren't they concerned about the Thai forces?"

"Who cares around here?" Tee-wah said.

"When can we go to see Thompson?" Wang asked.

"You can leave tomorrow," answered Tee-wah.

"Will you come with us?" Melinda asked him.

"No. These children are killers." He stepped closer to Melinda. "And you should not go. Kampuchea is a country of lies and great misfortune. You can't trust anyone. Even the foreigner who lives here is either bandit, thief, or beggar. Leave. For your own safety."

"Tee-wah," Wang said, soothingly.

Twenty meters away, several Khmer soldiers halted and gazed at us. Their smiles were gone, and they had fallen silent.

"You see?" Tee-wah said to me. "They hate you and men like Wang. Your life means nothing to them. And here in the hills who is there to speak of disappearances but the mountain ghosts?"

"I'm going on," Melinda said, returning to the shady ground beneath the tree.

That night, unable to sleep and with flashlight in hand, I walked through the village. A dog, hidden beneath one of the huts, snarled at me. Everyone slept. There were no lit lanterns or fires, and even the sound of my footsteps, smothered by the soft earth, were nonexistent. Ahead, I heard voices and snapped off my flashlight.

They were naked when I stumbled upon them. Through a parting in the brush, I saw the moonlight reflect off a village girl's arms and legs, her flat belly and small breasts. She walked toward a thickset boy, bent down and slid into his arms. It was Primo. He was on his knees, and she took him in her hand, as if it were an offering she could not refuse. He kissed her, and her lips pulled away from his mouth. When he laid her on the ground I crept away, hearing her faint cry, and followed the road to our sleeping quarters.

CHAPTER 17

AT DAWN, WANG and Primo led us over the bridge and down the mountain. Their backpacks were filled with supplies that Thompson had requested. Cast in shadow, the surrounding hills were tinseled with fog. Our boots glistened, coated with moisture, and the air smelled fresh. It was still early enough before the incoming heat and humidity. The walk took most of the day. Only once did someone speak, and that was Wang, pointing to the earth alongside the path, cautioning us of land mines.

By late afternoon with the sun an oval, fiery disc in the picture-blue sky a village appeared to our east. The outskirts of the village were made up of huts and two small-size military tents. Some items were in need of immediate repair, like the leaking water tank; the racks of ancient bicycles; the cratered road corrupted from land mines, aerial bombs, or artillery, and filled in with loose gravel and rock. Other objects were quite useless: a truck had been cannibalized, its parts, most probably, sold for scrap, and the truck transformed into a manure tank. A tractor, where children romped at the edge of a paddy, had the appearance of a dinosaur. It sat in the sun, rusted over and half hidden by vines. In the shade beneath the giant tractor, two dogs gamboled on the cooler ground.

Thompson's village appeared to be controlled by a small cadre of Khmer Rouge soldiers. A few sat in the shade smoking, while others watched from below their checkered *kramars*. Throwing off our packs, we rested beside a dead fire pit. No one in the village acknowledged us. Wang remained grim, requesting my silence with a shake of his head. Nearby, I noticed four men clad in military fatigue pants, boys really, and a slim teenage girl. She sat cleaning her rifle, the weapon dismantled on palm leaves; she used an oily substance in a Del Monte's peach can to grease its moving parts. I strolled over. She held the barrel to my eye for inspection. I nodded, smiling foolishly. It seemed, for some unfathomable reason, she wanted a Westerner's approval, or, more likely, to put fear in me, which she did.

I walked away and asked Wang who was the leader. He told me the soldier was called Long. Long had a mouthful of bad teeth, stained brown, and ate with the best utensils. But none were to be trusted. They were all flunkies.

"They'll steal your gold fillings," Wang said, "if you sleep with your mouth open. This is a damn poor country."

As we stood around the fire pit, my naive impression of them was not as soldiers but of armed children who belonged in school.

Melinda spotted Thompson first, pointing at an old man who possessed surprisingly good posture.

"Wang!" the old man called as he neared. "My son! Glad to see you!"

He shook Wang's hand and ignored Primo, who dug his boot heel into the dirt.

"Jim, these are friends of mine," Wang said. "Melinda. Sam. This is Jim Thompson."

"Call me father," Thompson said. "Or just Jim."

He was a slender old man who wore a black beret, black pants cinched with a rope belt, and Ho Chi Minh sandals. He had strong hands, like a laborer, long fingernails and thick wrists, which seemed his most prominent physical characteristic. His face was lined and weather-beaten. Oddly, his shirt had padding in the shoulders.

"This way," he said, taking Melinda's arm, directing us toward some earthen steps. "Leave your gear. My boy, Som, will take care of them."

Som swept out from behind Thompson, a pike-thin urchin who quickly gathered up our packs. With a huge smile, the boy tread at our heels.

Thompson lived on the other side of a wooden bridge. At its narrowest point, two convergent hillsides with vegetated rock faces towered over the bridge, while a shallow river, nicknamed the Snake, flowed lazily below the rickety suspension. The valley appeared as though it had been cleaved with a hatchet and leveled with a scythe.

Thompson's compound was more desolate and made up of fewer huts than the local village. Inside Thompson's hut were two wicker chairs, a round table, and a wooden platform that held a thin mattress. A bamboo shelf cradled several book volumes. Alongside the main room stood a kitchen with windows to allow for ventilation. On the kitchen shelves were plates, wooden bowls, two big metal pans, a few spoons and forks, and spices in clay jars.

Melinda and Thompson took the wicker chairs, while the rest of us sat on large floor pillows. The hut's wooden floor was clean and partially covered with two medium-size rugs.

"This is The Groaning Table Restaurant and Cocktail Lounge," Thompson said, as a white cockatoo landed on his shoulder. "It was a name journalists used at the Le Royal Hotel in Phnom Penh in the early seventies for briefings. This is before the Khmer Rouge took power." He placed the bird on a wooden bar near his bed. "It's good to see new faces. You've done well, Wang."

"Thank you, Mr. Jim."

Thompson rose and removed a small padlocked suitcase from beneath his bed. He used a key from his pocket, removed a palm-size sheet of gold from the suitcase, and handed it to Wang.

"This should cover what remains of your trip's expenses and the supplies."

"You're a noble man," said Wang.

Thompson locked the suitcase and sat back down.

"Excuse me," I said. "But are you Jim Thompson the famous silk entrepreneur from Bangkok who disappeared in the Cameron Highlands in Malaysia?"

"I am."

"The world thinks you're dead. Why are you here?"

"Are you a newspaper man?" Thompson asked. "I hate newspaper men."

"I'm here with Melinda because your man Wang said you have information about Melinda's mother."

Thompson looked at her and smiled. He was a cagey prankster.

"I remember you, child. I will tell you all you want to know." He placed his hands on his knees. "I left Thailand because I was unhappy. It wasn't the country I once loved, and it was changing in ways I didn't like. The Cambodians offered me the opportunity to live the life I wanted, a chance to return to a simple splendor. On my many visits to their country I often purchased artifacts, and so I easily became accepted in their society. I had often thought while in Thailand about leaving my life and possessions. It wasn't an easy decision, for many people relied on me, but I knew that in my absence my businesses and charities would be well managed. So, I arranged my disappearance. In those early years in Cambodia, I had my own hut, and each morning one of the workers brought me fresh cassava, which he roasted with rice.

"Four years later, the Khmer Rouge invaded my village. At first, they thought they would hold me for ransom. But Pol Pot, the political premier of the Khmer regime, decided against it. In the beginning I was treated like royalty. I became a famous loyalist of the Khmer Rouge." He stroked the thick white hairs of his left eyebrow. "Did you know that no one could wear eyeglasses during the Khmer Rouge regime? If you owned a pair, which I did, you were considered an intellectual. And if you wore them you were kaput--killed.

"When Pol Pot and his Khmer regime took power in Phnom Penh everything changed. The Khmer Rouge started their so-called re-education camps and murdered two million of their own people. Genocide. The word hasn't lost its fangs."

Someone had started a fire in the kitchen hearth. Smoky coils drifted through the room.

"Tell me about my mother," Melinda said, unable to mask her impatience.

Thompson dismissed her request a brief smile. "Later, my dear."

"So, you cared nothing about what the Khmer Rouge were doing," I said quickly.

The hostility in his blue eyes and the way he refused to answer Melinda disturbed me.

"I thought I wouldn't be harmed, and that I was superior to the peasants and the military. I was mistaken. Eventually, the Khmer treated me like all the other peasants and forced me to work in the fields. I was lucky I wasn't killed, being an obvious Westerner. We worked on projects. We built dams that were useless and always would be. They were constructed at improper levels, as if water could run uphill."

The old goat shook his head. All this reminiscing was tiring him. I had the impression he hadn't spoken of these things in a very long time.

"No one had any knowledge of engineering, especially the Khmer Rouge. The forced peasant labor was pointless and wasted. When the Vietnamese invaded Cambodia, I made my way to one of the Thai border refugee camps. I was starving like everyone else."

He inhaled deeply. "Ah, rice and curried meat. Supper will be delicious this evening," he said, as though the smells emanating from the kitchen alone were enough to satisfy him.

"I remember seeing Rosalyn Carter," Thompson said with a sigh, "the president's wife at Sa Kaeo camp on the Thai border in the fall of 1979. Famine was everywhere. Children and mothers died from starvation and disease after they emerged from the Cambodian jungle. But Western journalists swarmed around Rosalyn Carter in her white dress as if she were a nightingale. All they wanted was a picture. *Give me a photo, give me a photo* they kept chanting. And here these people were starving, sprawled on the ground, dead and dying."

His eyes narrowed, and the flesh at the tip of his chin wobbled. He stared at me. "You're American. Am I right?" I nodded. "It's a shame what your country did. After the Khmer Rouge were finally forced out of Cambodia by the Vietnamese, the Americans supplied the Khmer with weapons and food, just to oust the Vietnamese because they were Communists. The American government didn't care about two million Cambodians murdered and tortured to death. Men, women, and children. Only politics mattered."

"But you returned to Cambodia," I said.

"I have no other home, son."

He leaned over, stroked Melinda's cheek and ran his withered fingers down her arm.

"I've met you before, haven't I?" Thompson said. "Yes. That's it. I once knew your mother in Bangkok. A Chinese woman."

"Can you tell me about her?" Melinda asked, taking hold of his arm. "That's why I came to see you."

He placed his hand on top of hers. The scene, if it hadn't been murderously hot in the room, could have been spun from a Grimm's fairy tale.

"Daughter, I can tell you all you want to know. But first let's eat."

After the meal, Thompson complained of fatigue and told us he would meet with us tomorrow. He kissed Melinda good night, and his young urchin, Som, led us out of the compound and over the bridge to our quarters. Thompson lived isolated from the rest of the village.

Outside our hut, Melinda said to me, "He's wonderful. See? I told you he knew my mother."

"That's right," said Wang, patting his left breast pocket where he had stored his gold sheet. "He's a prince."

He winked at me and walked off. Melinda and I entered the hut where the coolness made me aware of how tired I was.

"We're leaving in the morning," I said.

"Stop it. He knows my mother. He said so."

She stood, with arms folded, just inside the hut below a wooden arch, which reminded me of a Japanese *tori*.

"She's dead. He said he knew her. *Thinks* he knew her. I don't trust him."

"Why don't you trust him?" Melinda asked. "Don't you want me to know about my mother?"

"He can only tell you lies. Tee-wah was right. We don't belong here."

"Don't talk like that. He knows my mother."

"Melinda, you're being used by Wang, Primo, and maybe Thompson, too. This isn't a pleasure trip for those two. They want the old man's loot.

They've conned you to play the part of his long-lost daughter to soften him up."

"I know," she said bitterly. "I'm just some Chinese cookie they hooked up with. I'm surprised you came along this far. What's in it for you?"

"Not a thing. Not a fucking thing."

She pressed her fingertips into her temples. Her voice lowered. "Why did you come, Sam? Was it for Jim's gold? You know, that would be all right if you say that, if it was for the gold. At least it wouldn't be something self-righteous." She sat down in the room's sole chair. "I wanted you to come, but not for me. I came here for my reasons, and if you said the gold I could understand that reason, even accept it."

"You got it. I came here for the gold."

"Good. Even that's better than coming just for me. But you won't harm him, will you? Promise me."

"Oh, I promise."

I hauled my backpack onto the bed, a tightly woven straw mat that would be ours for the next few nights, which we would share together for the first time in what seemed a great while. Melinda removed her boots, socks, and rubbed at a splotch of blood on her foot.

"Let me get some antiseptic and clean that off. Wounds infect easily here."

She spat on her palm and rubbed at the bloodied spot.

"Never mind. I can take care of myself."

For a time, I had ignored Melinda's growing lack of affection toward me and believed it was due to the heat and the lengthy journey.

I thought of her Master, her Buddha God. *Teach me to love again, to love her. Let us be happy.*

I was trying to pray. It had been so long. But supplication was not part of my field kit. I sat beside Melinda and placed her foot in my lap. A blister had broken and was leaking blood.

"It hurts," she said, softly. "I can hardly walk."

I removed the antiseptic crème from my backpack, wiped the toe clean with a sterile pad, and applied the crème and a Band-Aid.

"That feels good," she said.

We undressed and stretched out on the bed. She lay with her back to my chest, and we made love that way, but I wanted more from her that evening, more than this. I wanted the devotion she had given Thompson, so quickly and willingly.

CHAPTER 18

THE FOLLOWING EVENING I walked to the nearby river and stood just inside the woods. The trees, black statuesque trunks, were attractive and smooth to the touch, and the ground was sprinkled with light. The jungle scent filled my head. I wasn't afraid, and there was still enough daylight to see a short distance into the jungle. Minutes later, a young woman hobbled toward the river's bank. The area was deserted, and I watched her walk several meters in each direction to ensure her privacy. I was about to leave when she sat on the ground, pulled off her pants, and disconnected her left leg. Afterward, she removed her blouse and wrapped the synthetic limb in the white cloth.

I left, preserving her privacy. That night, after dinner, Thompson remained resistant to disclosing information about Melinda's mother. With Melinda unusually quiet, I mentioned to him the woman I had seen at the river.

"She has little hope of marrying," Thompson said. "Though with her artificial leg she looks normal. One can barely notice the limp. And she speaks English. I know she likes to sew. She's the best seamstress in the village. There are thousands of men, women, and children in Cambodia without limbs, who have hooks for arms. I'm sure you've noticed."

They were as much a part of the village as the scrawny dogs.

"Maybe she'll fall in love and her leg won't matter to the boy," Thompson said. "It doesn't matter to me. This is a country of artificial limbs."

"Is she your daughter?" I asked.

He nodded. His cockatoo was asleep on its wooden bar.

"Her name is Oung Yi, and she lost her leg two years ago in an explosion in a rice paddy. Countless people have lost their lives to the land mines. Many Cambodians who live along the Thai border refuse to return to their homes. The ground frightens them. How can you farm a country full of mines?"

"It's a terrible weapon," I said.

"Yes. It keeps on killing after the generals and the corporations call off their little wars. The latest technology makes these devices almost impossible to disarm. A Motorola chip will tell the mine to blow with any kind of movement. In others, when you disarm the top one the bottom one blows. Another will detonate as soon as it experiences a 15 percent tilt. The people are equally afraid of the bandits who rob the border camps."

"We didn't see the camps," Melinda said. "We must have come another way."

"You took the drug smugglers' route. Very beautiful but dangerous. I guess you had to. Otherwise, you may never have gotten here."

"We're thankful to Wang and our guide," Melinda said.

"Yes. I'm glad you made it here safely."

"Is there anything I can get you?' Melinda asked.

"My slippers. They're by my bed."

She retrieved them, knelt by his side, and placed the slippers on his feet. My stomach turned at this servile demonstration.

There was a knock on the door and words spoken in Khmer. Thompson answered, and Oung Yi walked in. She carried a basket of fruit, melons, and cassavas. A long yellow dress, faded from washing, fell past her knees. I looked at her feet. She was sockless and wore black shoes. Only a tiny glimpse of ankle gave away the artificial limb. No wood stain could match the attractiveness of her brown skin.

Thompson introduced us, and Oung Yi smiled.

"It's nice to meet you," I said, rising.

She spoke slowly. "Nice to meet you."

In Western style, she reached out and I shook her small, rough hand. After three shakes, she flipped my hand over and ran her fingertips over my palm. "So smooth," she said.

Her body was thin, and I could sense her frailty, the way one anticipates a summer cloudburst. But her grip was firm, the fingers long.

"You have child's hand," she said.

"Peasant hands," I said, "like my father. Thick and fatty."

A horseshoe scar, the size of a fingernail, marked her left eyebrow.

A moment later Thompson spoke in Khmer, the words clicking from the back of his throat at a rapid rate.

Oung Yi dropped my hand, glanced at Melinda sitting on the floor, and exited.

"Where's Oung Yi's mother?" I asked.

"Dead," said Thompson. "I've tried to make Oung Yi happy. She has much to live for if she'd only try. Like the *bomoh* says, we will return to the center." He took notice of Melinda's puzzled expression. "When a pebble is thrown into a pond, at first its circles move away from the center. That's what we do. But ultimately we return to the center. Like you have, daughter."

"She doesn't belong to you," I said.

"Please, Sam," Melinda said. "Don't start."

She looked saintly sitting by Thompson's feet, a woman beribboned with blue and yellow streamers which she wore on her blouse, a gift from either Thompson or Tee-wah. She appeared radiant.

"Tell me, Jim, who sent Oung Yi to the fields the day of her accident?"

"She went looking for watermelons. She knows how I like them."

"I'm sure she loves you," Melinda said.

"Are you Melinda's father?" I asked.

"I very well could be. She and Oung Yi look alike, don't you agree?" He folded his hands. "Do you believe in goodness of action, son?"

"Don't call me that."

"Do you believe in goodness of action? You can molest a child, am I right? Or pat him on the head. I'm not Western religious. I don't go to church. When I have an evil thought, I cast it out. I pluck out the rotten peg. That's goodness of action. I don't hurt people. Are you capable of that? Throwing out an evil thought, a selfish desire?"

"I'm no angel," I confessed, stepping up to him. "Now, if all you've said is true, if you want me to believe that you're Melinda's father, I can only assume you killed her mother. If not by your own hand then by your action. You either deserted her or took her here to live with you in a country not her own. However you look at it, where's your goodness of action now?"

"She poisoned herself. The dear girl. We can only pray for her now."

Melinda seized his knee. "Tell me more about my mother."

I sensed Thompson's lies and behind his gaze, deceit.

"She came to my house as a servant to work in the kitchen. She was a young woman of Chinese origins, flawless tan skin, bright eyes that would put the moon to shame. I knew immediately she didn't belong in the kitchen. She was educated and spoke four or five languages. Her meals were exquisite. In the evening, she massaged my shoulders after I had tended to my factories. We often played cards together, gin rummy. I can see her even now in her black silk blouse, her regal posture, and her eyes lifting away from the cards. She charmed me. Bedeviled me. Without my even noticing, she took charge of the house duties, the servants. She managed everything, including the monthly income I left at her disposal."

"How again did she come into your employ?" I asked.

He looked at Melinda. "Forgive me, daughter. I bought her. Such things were done in those days."

"Like a slave," I said.

"She became my queen," Thompson protested.

"How many others have you bought or sold?"

His reedy voice raised an octave. "I was the prisoner of the Khmer Rouge for three years. I was nearly executed. You can't begin to understand the horror of those days."

"You're right, I can't. And I wouldn't begin to try. Only Melinda and Melinda's mother concern me."

"And so it should."

"Are you her blood father?"

"Could be," he said, rather nonchalantly. "She was pregnant with Melinda when she worked for me. But there were others in her life."

"Man, answer the question."

Melinda stood up, visibly shaking. "Enough. You're talking about her as if she's dead. Well, is she truly dead?"

"All you need to know," Thompson said, "is that she had a good heart."

"I need to know more." Melinda placed her hand on Thompson's arm. "Please. Talk to me of her thoughts, beliefs, and dreams."

I moved toward the door and seized the handle. I didn't have the heart to listen any longer to what I believed were his deceptions.

"Stay, why don't you?" Melinda asked in a half-pleading voice.

"Do stay," Thompson echoed.

"To the devil with you," I said.

Outside, I sat near the raging fire pit where three Khmer soldiers were roasting a pig and drinking bottles of beer. I joined them. The girl, whose spotless weapon I had inspected earlier in the day, handed me a plate of meat. Walking out of the firelight, Oung Yi came closer and sat beside me.

"Hello. Is your friend okay?" Oung Yi asked. "She looks sad."

"She's searching for her mother," I said, moving the meat around with a spoon.

"I knew her mother from two, three years ago. A Chinese woman arrived, brought by Mr. Wang." She shook her head. "I don't like Mr. Wang or his friend. The woman stayed a short time. Father kept her hidden in another hut. I never spoke to her. Then one day she was gone."

"And why do you think she was Melinda's mother?"

"The eyes," Oung Yi said, flicking an ant off her wooden calf. "They look the same. But maybe I'm wrong. My father wouldn't have hurt her. He doesn't really like to hurt anyone."

I put the plate on the ground. "Has he ever hurt you?"

"He's a good man, my father. That's all you need to know."

"He said Melinda's mother died of poison. Did it happen here?"

She struggled to her feet, and I rose with her. "I don't know. It doesn't matter. There has been so much death in my country. A missing woman, who can care about someone long dead? We have to look after the living."

"That's what I'm trying to do. But Melinda won't leave without her mother or at least until she finds out about her."

"That woman is dead. That's all I know. They took her away and buried her. Whether she was Melinda's mother or no, I don't know. It is a bad thing to be haunted by the past. I feel sorry for her."

I touched her arm and she pulled away. "I need your help. How can I prove to her that that woman was her mother?"

"My father knows everything," Oung Yi said. "Make him tell her."

"How can I do that?"

"You have to find a way. She is pretty. Watch after her," Oung Yi warned.

CHAPTER 19

⟨✦⟩

THE NEXT DAY Thompson fell ill. Fearing for his health, Melinda arranged a straw floor mat and slept in his hut. She bathed him and took his meals on a silver tray to his bedside. In the cooler evening air, she read Buddhist texts to him by a kerosene lamp. I helped her when I could, taking away dishes, washing her clothes at the river. A determination had taken hold of her revealed by a tautness in her face, the loss of weight, a stillness in her body when she sat beneath a sugar palm tree.

On the fourth morning of Thompson's illness, Melinda spoke forcefully to me as I sat by the river's edge. She wore a sarong and stood hip-deep, bathing in the water.

"I won't leave him until he's better," she said. "When he's alert, he tells me of his early years in British Intelligence in World War II. Soon he'll speak of my mother. I'm patient."

"Ditto."

"I'm glad you understand."

She poured water from a wooden bowl over her head. She had never looked more beautiful.

"Is he going to die?" I asked.

"No. It's just a return of malaria he's had for years. It comes on him sudden sometimes." I noticed a sizeable scratch above her left breast and asked her about it. "Father did it. It was an accident."

But there was something in her tone that worried me. Recalling Oung Yi's words about Thompson hurting people, I wondered where else he had touched her.

"Sleep with me tonight. I miss you."

"Soon." She emptied water from the wooden bowl into the river. "He's getting better. I think he's always relied on people. I sense that weakness in him. He's helpless," she said, stepping out of the river. "I have to go now."

"Remember to write." She stood beside me. I gently clasped her ankle, and her hand went to my hair. "Wait. You're wet. Dry off in the sun."

"I want you to understand," Melinda said. "If I give up now, I'm lost. If I don't find out about my mother and who I am nothing will be right again. I'll never get my son back. I'll never be able to love you. A part of me will hate you. You see us being together in the future, don't you?"

"It's my plan."

"I wish I could believe that."

"Trust me."

"I don't care about marriage. I'd like to have a house someday with you and my son. That's my only dream besides finding out about my mother."

"And how does Thompson fit into the equation?"

Her fingers stroked my forehead. "He'll never leave this village. And we don't belong here. I know that." She paused, gazing down at me. "He talks of death and killings and women he has made love to. He's in his right mind, just a little feverish. But I think he does this to test me, to be sure I'm on his side for some reason."

"He has a motive," I cautioned her. "Don't be too open. Even Oung Yi is afraid of him."

"My sister?"

"She knows something about him that she can't talk about. She's dropped some hints to me, but nothing solid."

"I'm glad you've found a friend." Melinda looked toward the village. "He's waiting. Be good."

I watched her walk up the low hill into a torrid blue sky.

The next day I helped villagers build a new schoolhouse using brick and mortar. The construction had been intermittent due to the heat and periodic lull in materials brought in from Phnom Penh, the capital. On this day fresh brick had arrived, and I joined several men and women in the labor. Oung Yi remained closeby, acting as my interpreter and historian. During lunch, she explained the ancestry and disintegration of village families, gesturing toward a certain man or woman at the site, recounting their story of loss or their journey to return home.

Oung Yi gestured toward a rain-thin boy. Than was in his late teens and had been blinded in one eye by a land mine explosion. When Than was ten, a Khmer Rouge soldier had tricked three boys of the village with promises of American sweets to go into a rice paddy to search for undesirables, supposedly hiding in the paddy. The soldier waited in a nearby field, smoking. Soon the land mine detonations began, and while the other boys were killed, Than survived.

Within a couple of days the building supplies extinguished. The following morning, with nothing to do, I asked Oung Yi if I could meet Than. His story intrigued me. In the village, he was known for his ability to ferret out dangerous land mine regions. Often he guided refugees over the nearby Dangrek Mountains to the safety of the village. At my insistence she agreed to introduce us. That afternoon Oung Yi and I met Than at the river. He was bathing, his dwarfish body floating on the muddy surface. He wore Raybans with the Rayban sticker stuck to the glass over the spot where his right eye used to be.

He coasted onto the pebbly shore. Rising onto his elbows he snorted, and from his nose blew a load of phlegm onto the ground.

He yawned and talked in Khmer.

"He says he's blessed," Oung Yi explained. "The eye is his good omen. But he's a nut for believing that. When he gets too smart the soldiers will kill him."

"Ask him if he knows Melinda's mother. And does he remember the woman who was here a couple of years ago."

She nodded. Than remained floating in the stream, holding onto a boulder. A whimsical smile appeared on his face. He spoke quite boldly and loudly.

"He has no idea what you're talking about." She paused and looked at me. "People think that one always remembers those who die. But that isn't so. People want to forget; they want to go on living. But if he did know he would tell you."

"Why are you so certain he'd tell me?"

She shook her head. "You're American. You're like a god to him."

Then Than spoke.

"He wants to know if he can have your wristwatch."

"No."

He spoke again. "He said you can go with him tonight if you want. He's leaving to find some lost refugees from the Wat Ko camp near the Thai border and guide them here. They're most likely heading toward one of the old mine fields, not far from the temple of Preah Vihear. Maybe he'll remember something of what you want to know."

Than nodded and held up his wrist, his smile beaming.

Each night I slept alone and my dreams grew more disturbing. In the dreams, or so I thought, I saw Tee-wah just above the forest line of the village, having progressed between the mine fields into Cambodia. He advances, as if having crossed a harsh sea, bone tired from his lengthy journey. Melinda is at the edge of the jungle, brown as the tree bark. He approaches her, slowly, too weary to raise his arm and wave, a fearless man whom I have no weapon against. His hands reach for her, seize her waist, remove her skirt, and he makes love to her. They are oblivious to all, the animals, the peasants working in the rice paddy, the eyes of the jungle, the coming darkness that settles over them like a shroud. He ruthlessly explores her body with his hands; he is inside her, and this does not disturb me. It is only when I see her place her hand on his face, around his chin, the way a mother does to her child, a caress as natural as rain, that I know he is my enemy and I am powerless to stop him.

I removed my wristwatch and tossed it to Than. Perhaps this trek into the countryside would rid me of my sleepless nights and unpleasant dreams. Than held up two fingers in the shape of a V.

That evening, as I waited for Than at the edge of the village, I saw Melinda exit our hut wearing her favorite hat, a blue beret. On bad days of fighting between the Khmer Rouge and the Cambodian military, she wore her beret, a magical derby which she believed protected her from the snipers' bullets, and the snipers who took random potshots at whomever crossed the bridge. The shooting appeared to be a game to the military. Sometimes we could hear their laughter echo from the hillsides.

Melinda crossed, untouched. I shouted encouragement. She didn't hear me and doggedly took the bend that led to Thompson's hut.

A half hour later, Oung Yi advanced up the small hill. It was twilight, and a hazy redness settled over the land.

"Are you going with the Khmer Rouge?" she asked me.

"Yes, I am."

A warm breeze blew her hair off her face. She momentarily grabbed my shirtsleeve. "You should not go. The Khmer Rouge will kill you. They've killed so many."

"I'll be fine," I told her. "I'm going to help these people from the refugee camp. That's all. There won't be any dangerous Khmer Rouge, except the ones from this village, and they're harmless."

She laughed closed-mouth at my innocence. "They killed my husband. They will kill you too. Your white skin means nothing here. There's a price on your long nose. The Khmer hate the Sihanouk government."

"All that's in the past. The execution brigades are gone. Even Thompson speaks that way. The Khmer Rouge are dead and dying. Pol Pot has passed on. There's even talk in Phnom Penh of a democratic government."

"You believe too easily in such words."

"Western newspapers aren't owned by the government. They tell the news honestly. Your country is getting better. What happened in the past is sad and terrible, but it's over."

A breeze fanned the jungle trees, and a moistness pressed itself against my neck.

"Excuse me, but where do you belong?" Oung Yi asked.

I stared at her. "That's a silly question."

"Why silly when one's place is what mostly determines a person's life path. Good or bad. Look at me. I'm maimed. This village, these fields, Kampuchea has fashioned me. I am not formally educated. I was taught by missionaries. Tell me, do you think people have to be of the same country to be together?"

"No, they don't."

"So someone like you and me is possible...in your country?"

"Quite possible."

"If not for Melinda."

I meant to touch her long fingers, but a continent divided us, and my own cowardice.

"Where do you belong?" I asked.

"In this spot, right here, with you," she said.

"At this moment there is no other place for me either."

She seemed pleased by this.

"But if you had a wish, where would you want to live?" I asked.

She smiled. "Now *that* is a silly question. I can go nowhere else. So I never ask myself that question."

"You should."

"You mean it's something you ask yourself?"

"I have. Some people are fixed in a spot and like it. Most people, I think, want a quiet life. Except for holiday, they remain at home. They are grounded in a country, a city, or village. They stay and find some place that satisfies them. I've never had that sense of place, that kind of satisfaction for any period of time."

"Maybe that is your satisfaction. Like the wind unable to find a place to rest."

"That's poetic. But I don't think so."

The land had turned the color of burgundy, and the sun on the horizon appeared to be a molten pool.

"And that's why you go with Than tonight because you're bored?"

"No. That's not it. Let me explain. Years ago, I read a book by the writer Carlos Castaneda. In this book, the main character took a drug called peyote. For pages and pages Castaneda describes this man walking on his porch, settling temporarily in one spot after another. Each time the man rested, he hoped to find the *right* place for him on the porch. And each time he rose to his feet, dissatisfied. He continued to walk around his porch, rest, searching for the place where he belonged on the porch. In the end, he sat on the floor, even though it felt wrong. Castaneda never explains why the man chose this particular spot on the porch. These days I feel like that man."

"Was the man alone?" Oung Yi asked.

"Yes."

"It would have been much better if he was with someone. Then the spot wouldn't have mattered."

Lanterns were lit in several huts, giving the village a friendly radiance.

"I have to go," I said.

She shook her head. "You're a nut to do this."

"Look after Melinda. I'll be fine."

"Follow Than and listen to him. Don't be brave on the trail."

She left without issuing another warning. As she limped away, she held up two fingers, stunned, perhaps, by my recklessness and equally per-plexed by my motive. *How easy it is to die in this land.* She must have thought that. I did. What use could I be on this expedition? I was excess baggage, a handicap. Oung Yi was right. One's skin color or belief means nothing in a country sown with land mines.

CHAPTER 20

⸺ ❦ ⸺

WE DEPARTED BEFORE darkness settled over the village. Than, the Khmer soldier girl, two of her comrades, and myself, made up a taut squad heading northeast. The moonlight mapped a visible path.

We walked for hours in silence, maintaining a singular formation along the trail, heading toward the rising moon. The air remained close, humid, without a breeze. It was difficult to catch one's breath. There were no bird calls or animal sounds. At one point, Than stopped and the Khmer soldier girl departed, scurrying into the jungle. I looked at Than and he placed his hands together below his chin, as in prayer. Curious, I went into the jungle after the Khmer girl. Within a minute, I found her. She was down on her knees, praying before the Lord Buddha. The statue was made of stone and stood ten feet high. Flowers, burnt-out joss sticks, and offerings of rice and fruits lay before him. I stood at the edge of the temple grounds. The area had a feeling of holiness. I looked up into Buddha's noble, peaceful face said my prayers, backed away, and returned to our small squad. A short time later, the Khmer soldier girl joined us on the path and we continued forward.

An hour later, after we climbed a minor hillock, we stopped. Than gestured at a field no more than fifty meters ahead, and at the path that wove through brush, which led toward a mountain range. My breathing was ragged. With my shirtsleeve, I wiped sweat from my face and gulped water from my canteen.

Than touched my shoulder. "Boom!" he said.

He stared at the field and at a string of distant lights against the mountainside. His finger tapped the illuminated number eleven on his watch face.

Suddenly, the Khmer girl went by us in a huff, leaving the other two soldiers smoking beneath a Banyan tree. In a shrill voice, she yelled in Khmer at the long peasant line, as the lanterns continued to advance.

Than left, moving soundlessly along the path, his squat frame in pursuit of the Khmer soldier girl. I followed on his heels. The reedy stalks were waist-high and the air, due to the untended field, smelled faintly of coffee. I ran at half-speed, aware of the danger on either side. Within minutes, the refugees were visible. A child, holding a lantern, led the small band. She had been chosen to lead them. It was as if her soft footfalls might dissuade the land mines from detonating. The simple fact that the child was in front was a startup kit for lunacy.

When she saw the Khmer soldier girl, the child ran toward her. A woman, her mother I assumed, directly behind her, struggled to keep up. Seconds later I heard a big sound. Somewhere in the middle of the line, one of the refugees had set off a land mine. The child turned and stepped sideways off the trail, awed by the noise and the violent expression of the land. Her lantern, swinging to and fro, was momentarily stilled, and then she and the lantern light disappeared in a loud explosion. The mother was next, blindly walking into the field after her daughter, leveled by mud and metal. Moving off the path, the Khmer girl raced toward the child. After that the refugees went down like bowling pins.

In an instant, the Khmer soldier girl flew into the air, thrown to my left by the blast of a detonated mine. She had let her humanity get in the way of her job. The child she had gone to help was dead. The mother, too. They had both been blown to pieces. She must have known that. Their body parts were everywhere.

Than and I quickly reached the refugees, their screams and squabbling voices reverberating all around us. Scattered in the field, people were dying and crying out for help. I was glad I couldn't see them all. Most of the lanterns had been destroyed, flung away or smashed by the mines' concussions. I went forward, off the path and into the field. The Khmer girl lay on her back. Her arms were gone, and one boot had been blown off her foot. Her body trembled as if terribly cold, and she said something in a language I didn't know. I grabbed her weapon, which was nearby but badly damaged, and placed it against her torso. She smiled oddly as she died, a pitiful smile, in fact, as if somehow I had done the most awful thing, when all I had wanted was to appease her and give her a final pleasure, like placing a favorite doll beside a child at bedtime.

Afterward, I helped carry the injured to a small, safe clearing, dragging a few who bit and clawed me, wanting to return for a relation or loved one dead or wounded in the field. After I carted them away from the mine field, they lay on the ground like puppies. A few prayed. Others were silent. Many cried. I never knew the living could wail so loudly over the dead. Twice I walked foolishly into the field, the first time to check out a hand waving, and the second toward a baby someone held up in the air. Both times I could do nothing but leave.

Up the path a man lay face down. I walked ahead and picked him up, my fingertips against his ribs, an old skinny gent who placed his vile lips on my neck.

"Now, now," I said, pinching his nose, and swinging it away as he limped alongside me, my arm around his waist.

In the clearing, I dropped him beside a young girl who cradled a baby in her arms. The place was thick with refugees. The healthy ones had already begun to walk up the trail. Those who remained were stretched out on the ground or propped up against trees, checking their wounds or simply physically wasted. I could no longer hear screams or shouts from the field. A few stragglers limped toward me. Than was one of the last. When he reached us, he spoke loudly in an agitated voice at the refugees, flailing his arms and pointing down the trail. Slowly people began to rise, hauling up their bundles, helping others less fit.

I put my arm around the old man's waist, and we trudged up the trail. He smelled of shit and piss and weighed no more than a bundle of sticks. His hands and chest were bloody. The girl walked ahead of us, holding her silent baby to her chest. When the old man moaned, she turned her head and spoke harshly to him in Khmer. Responding, he shook a twig-like arm at her and mumbled some pathetic response into my ear. Soon he began to cry. I lifted him up and carried him for a kilometer or two until we reached a calmer region. The two male Khmer soldiers had not followed. The last I saw of them they were stripping the gear from their dead comrade.

"What about the other wounded?" I asked Than.

We had stopped for a brief rest. He was on his knees bandaging a man's leg. He looked up at me. His glasses were off, the vacant socket moist with tears.

Thirty minutes later, we moved out. On the trail, the old man and the girl walked in front of me. Nestled in her arms, the baby was wrapped in cheap red cloth. Now and again the girl kissed the child's forehead, the only exposed portion in the red cloth. We marched. No one spoke. The moonlight was bright, lighting the trail. I stared straight ahead, avoiding the jungle darkness on either side.

Only once did someone speak to me, and that was the old man who mumbled a few unintelligible words and gestured with arthritic fingers for me to take the baby. The girl held the child tightly, so tightly that it frightened the old man. What did it matter? Let her keep him. Still, the old man moved ahead and took the bundle from the girl, who released the child, reluctantly. Oddly, her shoulders sagged, and her arms folded below her breasts, as if a much greater weight had been placed there. The old man stopped and thrust the bundle into my hands. It was as though I held a bag of stones. The baby had that kind of gravity. I peeked at its face, readjusted my forearm along its slim dead body, and gently turned its head into my chest.

"It's okay," I said to the girl and the old man. "Tell her it's okay. I've got him now."

I don't know the time we entered the village, but the moon was a little past its zenith in the night sky. The girl retrieved her dead baby from me and joined the refugees who were ushered off to another section of the village. I stood near the fire pit, still alive with glowing embers and felt its slow heat on my arms. From out of the darkness, Oung Yi came toward me. She limped badly.

"It's very late," she said, standing beside me.

With her good foot, she pushed a burning ember back into the fire pit and a small flame twisted.

"I don't like to sleep," she said. "I fight it. My dreams are full of voices. Faceless voices and words I can't remember."

"Are you hurting?" I asked, gesturing to her artificial limb.

"I need to go to Phnom Penh and have my leg repaired."

I reached into my pocket and handed her some Thai baht notes. She took the money without debate.

"Sometimes I dream I have two legs again, and I run freely in the rice fields feeling the grass under my toes. I really wish my friends and I can play without danger and there are no more mines in our fields. It's a child's dream I have of looking at the ground and seeing two brown feet. The United States is the leading mine manufacturer in the world. They kill and hurt so many of my people with their mines. Don't your people know what they do?" She looked at the exposed wooden ankle. "They say this is the Rolls Royce of artificial legs." She touched my arm and said, "Many died."

I nodded. She moved closer to me.

"They won't allow me to love. Why not?"

"Who won't allow you?"

"They."

"And who are they?"

I heard gunfire in the hills and wondered who the soldiers might be shooting at in the dark.

"You know. The men."

"What men, Oung Yi?"

"The men of my country."

"And these men," I said, "do they love you?"

"Once I could sleep with a man, hold him and believe the words he said by the look in his eyes. But now the eyes tell nothing, are nothing, and all words are lies."

She looked down the dirt road toward Thompson's compound, glanced in the other direction and walked off.

Soon afterward I burned my clothes. I knew the blood wouldn't launder out. Moreover, I wanted to see the shirt scorched, my pants, too. I watched as they flamed to ash, as if I could burn the memory. When they caught fire, I was surprised at how little I felt. I touched a welt on my rib cage. My body was scratched, sore, black and blue. It was as though it had been flattened in a wrestling ring.

Inside my hut I pulled a small bone from my boot and chucked it outside. I didn't know whose it was, and I would have buried it, honest to God. I would have given it its proper resting place, but I was too near exhaustion to care.

CHAPTER 21

PEOPLE VANISH AND no questions are asked. I found this true the following morning. No one spoke about the field, the land mines, or the dead. The refugees tried to establish themselves by going into the village, gathering information and food. The scuttlebutt was that a detachment of Khmer Rouge from the Wat Ko camp were in pursuit to collect an unpaid duty from the refugees. According to Oung Yi, many people, villagers and refugees alike, upon hearing the rumor, prayed that the land mines would multiply like locusts eating the Khmer Rouge soldiers.

As I stood near the bridge, the old man I had helped ambled by me without a word. He had attached himself to a family and had become their adopted sage or grandfather. Than was no longer in the village. In the afternoon, I saw a girl cleaning her weapon and mistakenly took her for the Khmer soldier girl I had seen killed.

At dusk, I went down to the river to get away from the crowded village. I stood beside some wild weeds drinking in the sweet, rich smell. Moments later I spotted Oung Yi, but I stepped into the jungle brush to escape her from seeing me. She exercised the same routine I had seen before, her cautionary walk in each direction, assessing her privacy. When she was satisfied, she sat down on the river bank, removed her shoes and her artificial limb and placed them on a boulder, safe from the river. I was tempted to make my presence known, but a stronger force kept me silent. I marveled at her determination. It was the way she moved without her artificial limb that mesmerized me, so unlike the beggars I had seen on Bangkok streets, holding plastic cups, some armless, legless, half-limbs covered with soiled bandages. Oung Yi had grace.

The light was golden. The river moved over rocks and beat against the shore. She stripped and placed each article of clothing beside the limb. When she was naked, she edged her body over the muddy soil into the river until the water swirled around her waist. She held a bar of soap and began to wash her neck, arms, and breasts. She splashed herself clean, raised the stump and soaped her brown skin and the stitch lines that covered the severed bone. She lathered the other leg, feeling in-between her toes, admiring the painted toenails. Curling her leg beneath her, she raised herself and washed her belly and below. Her black hair was loose and wet from a brief dunking. She gazed at the current, the way it cut into her body.

Abruptly her body stiffened, and she hurriedly dragged herself from the river. Her fingers fumbled with her skirt as she sat in the hard mud. Someone neared. She knew she had little time, not enough. Several refugees heading to another section of the river walked past, oblivious to the woman on the river bank. Still wet from the river, she struggled briefly with her limb. After it was secure, she trundled home.

As the sun went down the river turned black. I thought Oung Yi might return to finish bathing, so I waited and moved nearer the river. She didn't, and as I made my way over a small rise that led toward the village, I saw a woman in a beret exit the jungle.

"How's Father?" I asked Melinda the next morning.

It was a term she used when referring to Thompson. It seemed inappropriate. I believed Thompson wasn't her legitimate father. To diminish his status, I withheld the personal pronoun *your*; cursing him, I thought to make the word seem less real. All it did, I think, was heighten him in her eyes.

The sun was up, the sky cloudless, a searing blue. We stood next to the quiet fire pit, waiting for coffee that the urchin Som brought us each morning.

I huddled in my two shirts against the morning chill. Som arrived with the hot coffee.

"He wants me to live with him permanently," Melinda said, blowing on the steaming coffee.

The face carries everything, every pain and death, regret and tragedy, whirlpool of betrayal, as well as love, and one's failures. Melinda's face looked calm.

"And what do you want to do?" I asked.

"I thought I knew but now I'm not sure."

"Listen to me. He's alone. And I don't blame him for that. But he wants you to keep him company under this lie that you're his long-lost daughter. What rubbish. And even if you are, you'll die if you stay here. He'd like that, the way he killed the woman he said is your mother."

"Don't you think Oung Yi and I look alike?"

"Yes."

"She's my sister."

"Maybe. But ask Oung Yi. See if she wants you to stay. She has no one. She'll tell you the truth."

Melinda placed the toe of her foot on my boot.

"Father isn't lying," she said in a soothing voice. "He shouldn't be alone. He's old and could die any time. It's just that I don't want to have regret. And if I leave him, I'm worried that I'll be deserting him, and I know I'll never see him again."

"He's blackmailing you."

"Yes. In a way. If I promise I'll stay, he'll tell me all the stories about my mother. But you can go. I don't want you to be hurt."

I placed two fingers on Melinda's slim forearm. "What do you talk about all day?"

"Sometimes he tells me stories about my mother when she was young. I know not all the stories are true, but I believe even the make-believe ones."

"Why?"

"There's some truth in everything, isn't there?"

"Tell me one."

She slid her arm free from my fingers. Finally she said, "I'll tell you the story the way Father told me, like it's actually happening. My mother is twelve years old and a housekeeper for a rich Chinese family. She's been a housekeeper for two years and will stay a housekeeper for five more years. She cleans, makes beds, and earns a dollar a month. Her bed is the floor, and each night she sleeps with a pillow and blanket wrapped around her body. She's a virgin girl, though the lord of the house has tried to seduce her. When she runs away at seventeen, she's hired as a dancer in a bar, and two weeks later a Japanese man pays ten dollars to the bar owner and she goes off with him. It is her first time with a man. She lives in one room with four other girls and one of the girl's auntie and uncle. All the girls are dancers and go out with customers if the customer pays the bar. So, sometimes she sleeps with her girlfriends and sometimes she sleeps in fancy hotels or fleabag hotels with fat men and angry men and lonely men and men who just want to use her. Once or twice she falls in love. She is very young, and it is easy for her to fall in love with one of these men who shows the slightest kindness. But the men never stay long, a week or two. They have their fun, and my mother is back dancing in the same bar and sleeping with men she does not love or even like in hotels whose names and rooms she knows very well. But she earns more money than she ever thought possible.

"One day she receives a letter from her father, a farmer on a distant province, and he tells her that he needs money for a water buffalo. His old buffalo is dead. He explains he needs a new one for the planting season. My mother doesn't have a lot of money. Maybe seventy dollars. Six month's worth of saving. She asks the man she sleeps with, a man she has fallen in love with, a Westerner with green eyes to help her, and he refuses.

"'It's my problem' she says, 'my problem.' My mother stays with him for a week, and she doesn't talk about it again. She love this man, but soon he goes, and her problem remains."

Melinda stopped. Som refilled our cups, and we sipped quietly.

"What happened?" I asked.

"She never got the money. Her father didn't get the water buffalo. My mother continued to dance in the bar. You know, it's the way of life. The Westerner she loved wrote her letters but never returned. Afterward, there were other men who made promises, but they were always empty vows. One day she up and quit. A man had hit her and frightened her with his hands. She was just nineteen and had been in the bar for nine months. Soon her money was gone, and she was homeless, living on the streets, and pregnant. The child wasn't the Westerner's, this man she loved, but a Chinese guy, a drifter who took her to a motel where the water smelled bad."

Melinda paused and swallowed more coffee.

"She never saw the Westerner again. My mother was broke. Everyone avoided her. But one day a girl she once knew from the clubs met her on the street and took her in. The girl ran a clothes shop and my mother started to work for her. The child died a few days after birth.

"This is what my mother told Father. She spoke very little of her early days. But she wanted him to know this, for him to understand that she had been broken when she was young and may still be broken inside but she was also made of steel, because here she was in a nice home in Bangkok washing floors for a man who was her lover and who took care of her."

For some reason, Melinda appeared smaller each day. Her shoulders seemed shrunken, her body terribly thin. Like a jackal over its prey, bit by bit Thompson was devouring her.

"And when did she meet Thompson?" I asked.

Melinda shrugged.

"And where were you born?"

"Thailand. In his house. Jim told me that and I believe him."

"Is your mother alive?"

I don't have any more answers. I wish I did. But I don't."

I bent to kiss her, but she turned her face from me.

"I want you to eat more," I said.

She smiled, tickled my ribs, and sauntered off to Thompson's compound.

CHAPTER 22

AT NOON, MELINDA returned to our hut for her usual pre-supper nap. She headed directly for the sleeping mat, clearly exhausted. She paused briefly, kissed me on the cheek, and lay down, facing the bamboo wall. I was tempted to check her body for further abrasions or scratches. Before she rolled onto her side, I had glimpsed a blemish on her cheek. Was it from an insect bite? Or, had Thompson lashed out at her for some deranged reason?

While she slept, I made my way to the bridge that led to Thompson's compound. The bridge was made of wood and rope and had been reinforced with steel cable. No vehicles crossed the bridge, for it couldn't hold such weight, but it easily supported a squad of men carrying supplies or cattle moving between the two areas. Below the bridge, large boulders were visible in Snake River, and there was the smell of stagnant water in the slowly moving flow. Men and boys stood thigh-deep with nets in the middle of the river, hoping to catch the evening's meal.

There were no sentries or Khmer soldiers in Thompson's compound. Compared to the village, the area seemed deserted. I quickly found Thompson outside his hut, bathing his feet in a rubber tube of water made from old truck tires. He sat in a plastic chair beneath the leafy branches of a large rosewood tree watching children play European football in an old mine field. I observed him from a reasonably safe distance. He waved gaily at the children and hollered something in Khmer. The children halted their game, shouted back, and resumed playing. A moment later, Wang walked past me. I was unsure whether he had seen me or not, but he made no acknowledgement of my presence. He crouched low beside the old man. Thompson, as if dealing with a servant, placed his hand on Wang's head, gently massaging Wang's dark hair.

I was too far away to make out their conversation. When Wang lifted his gaze, Thompson's face grew drawn and he jammed his hand into Wang's forehead, pushing him away. Wang tumbled backward, stood, and walked toward the large water pitcher beside Thompson. He picked it up and dumped the contents onto the ground.

After flinging the pitcher away, he pointed at Thompson and shouted, "You think I've stolen from you! Incredible. It's you who deserves to have your hands amputated for all your misdeeds. You owe me. Never forget that. I haven't told your guests anything, but I will. If you don't pay me, I promise you I'll tell all." He spat on the ground and strode away.

I wasted no time and marched up to Thompson. He motioned me beside him to the same benign posture as Wang. I refused that post and sat opposite him on a large tree root.

"It's a pleasure to see you, Sam. I heard about your little adventure with Than. Now you know a small part of the dangers of this country. Maybe you see it's time for you to leave."

"Maybe it's time Melinda and I both left."

He jerked his foot in the rubber tube and splashed me. "Ho-Ho. My daughter isn't about to leave me yet. She's a lovely child. She wouldn't desert her father, and she cares so much for you she wouldn't want to see you accidentally injured. She knows what you did. She thinks as I do that your trek to Preah Vihear was idiotic. What I would give to be your age again."

"I'm not a young man."

He laughed. "Shut up. You have forty years of life ahead of you. Unless you piss it away by walking down jungle paths. Come here."

He motioned me nearer. "Please, please," he pleaded. I pushed myself off the root, strode up to him, and crouched so that we were of equal height. Without warning, he seized my ear, twisting it so that the pain forced me to my knees. He brought my face close to his, so that I smelled his odious breath and saw up close the offal skin. "No one will get in the way of me and my daughter," he said. "Not you or Wang. She's all I have left."

He released me. I cupped my ear and moved back to the tree root.

"And what did Wang want?" I asked, rubbing my ear.

"He wants only money and would sacrifice anything or do anything for it. I've known for years his motive for staying here. He's easy to read, like Melinda. She wants her poor dead mother to come back to life. And what do you want for yourself? Speak."

The words came from the dark, desolate place inside me, but I felt neither regret nor shame, only a sense of gratification after I spoke, as if slaying a mythical goblin.

"I want you to tell Melinda the truth about her mother and her childhood. And then be rid of you forever."

"Don't worry, son. My death will occur before long."

"Tell me, what's going to happen to Oung Yi? Will you discard her like you did Melinda's mother?"

"You should take Oung Yi away from here and see to it she has a better life."

"She'll never leave."

He closed his eyes and breathed deeply. His mouth changed from a slight grin to a frown, as if the thought he had seized upon had soured to disdain and settled upon a realization of all he had forfeited and lost. He looked at me and said, "I bathed her when she was a child. I saw her grow up. I know all her stories. I know what her life will be if she stays. Don't you want to give her a chance at a good life? Here she'll either end up being someone's mistress or go to Phnom Penh and be a two-dollar whore for the military."

"She's educated."

"This is Cambodia. Out here, what good is missionary education?"

"You should take care of her."

"In Southeast Asia the children take care of the parents when they're old. Oung Yi knows this is our way. You know it, too. Throw your Western rules away. Man, how did you ever expect to keep Melinda? She's Asian. Like Oung Yi, she knows her obligation." He leaned back in the chair and straightened his legs. The tops of his toes perched above the tube's rim.

"I know your father's dead. That he died when you were a boy. Melinda told me. It doesn't matter how old one gets, we're all still children. Even old men want to speak to their fathers. And if men can't recall their father, they want to invent one or have a friend and treat him like one. They want to bare their souls, even to cry. They want to confess, idolize, and ask for advice. That's what you want, isn't it? You want my guidance, my help. It's the reason Melinda came here. She's not following a ghost. I know that's what you think. In fact, she's wants someone to love."

"And she found you."

"I am the lucky one." He took a shallow breath. "Now, help me clean up." He removed the towel from the chair's arm and held it out to me. "Be a good person. Dry my feet. The heat is awful today, and I need to go to my hut and lie down."

"The feeble act is a good touch," I said. "I bet Melinda reacts well to it."

"I'm not acting. Help me."

"Now I understand why Oung Yi thinks you're dangerous."

"What are you talking about?"

I rose, took the towel from him and knelt beside the tube. As I lifted his left foot from the water, he asked, "Does Oung Yi really think I'm dangerous?"

I dried the foot, slipped his sandal on and did the same for his right foot. It pleased me he wanted information I had.

"She doesn't trust you. You've hurt her in some way, haven't you?"

"I've always treated her lovingly. She's a special woman. No one else cares for her like I do."

"You did something to her once, much worse than sending her out for cassava when she lost her leg. She's afraid of men, afraid of you, me, and her husband who abandoned her. Why is that?"

He rose and shook his fist at me. "You know nothing about us! Mind your own business and stay away from my daughter!"

He strode off and entered his hut. Before I left, his window shutter opened. The noise of a fan reached me and the air smelled of incense. His face appeared in the open window, and he jerked his head for me to come. I went forward and stood more than an arm's length from him. He wasn't going to hook me twice with his nasty fingers.

"What else has she told you?" he asked.

"Oung Yi?"

"Damn it," he said in a whisper. "Of course."

"Everything."

"I don't believe you. She doesn't love you. You've slept with too many whores in your life to know true love and innocence. I see that in your face." He smiled ingenuously. "She'll never let you near her. She *sees* better than me and knows the kind of man you are. The good Cambodian girls won't do anything until they're married. The only people they trust are their parents. The same goes for Melinda. There's so much she hasn't told you. The body and the spirit are distinctly separate. And I possess both of my daughters in a way you never can. I think it's time you left this country."

"And what does Wang know about Melinda's mother? Maybe I should speak to him?"

"He has only guesses. Only I know the truth, and that truth is for Melinda."

"Then tell her already."

"It's not very pretty. That's why I haven't told her."

"Tell me."

"Men like you are not to be trusted. In the end, even if you knew the truth, you'd lie to her to serve yourself. You view things in terms of ownership. I no longer have that luxury. For me, there are only memories and friendship."

He brushed a wisp of white hair from his forehead and disappeared into the hut. For several minutes I remained in that spot, beneath a monstrously hot sun, trying to figure out what dimension of Melinda I had failed to capture.

CHAPTER 23

THE REST OF the day hung empty. The fields were brown, untended. Many of the refugees had left, returning the village to its quiet attitude. Mothers and children sat in the windless huts, with doors propped open, shutters unlatched. A toy, a long wooden pole with a tiny wheel at one end, which the children wheeled up and down the dirt patches, was left abandoned in the road. In a nearby hut, a woman was threshing rice, the sound like the slow pumping of an oxen heart. It was the worst drought in twenty years.

I sat in the shade of a large tree, waiting out the day's heat, and watched a few peasants cross and recross the bridge. With each figure, I hoped to see Melinda. I tried not to think of how Thompson touched her, where he placed his hands and lips on her body, how he complained of the heat, cajoling Melinda, no doubt, in an avuncular tone, for her to disrobe.

I fell asleep for a short while. When I woke the fields and rice paddies were covered in an orange light that streamed evenly from the lowest quarter of sky, and the hut's shadows stretched across the road in narrow strips. My limbs were rubbery, and stones and twigs bruised my bare arms and neck.

Shortly, Oung Yi emerged from her hut, directly across from where I sat. She stood in a patch of sunshine, supported by Melinda, squinting against the dusk. She hadn't put on her artificial limb, and something red like blood had darkened the front of her skirt. Her hands were filthy, and her blouse buttons had been poorly fastened, as if in haste. Dried mud clung to her hair. Her bosom rose and fell as she weaved in Melinda's grasp.

Not twenty yards away, Primo sat on a rock observing an army of ants crawl over his left boot. For some odd reason he was heavily clothed. He wore a shirt, a sweater, an unzipped jacket, and he had tied a bandanna around his neck.

Oung Yi turned her gaze to Primo and whispered into Melinda's ear. Melinda nodded and called into the hut. A man emerged. He was Cambodian, a young civilian, hairless face and chest, scarecrow skinny like the ones that populated their fields, and smoking a cheroot.

The man, Oung Yi's cousin I learned afterward, walked up to Primo, withdrew his *parang* from his belt, and with one swing, cut off Primo's head.

Primo's body crumpled to his left side. His head rolled into the under-growth. I edged out of the shade and walked up to the limp carcass. My stomach felt ready to heave; I had never seen so much blood. A dog sniffed a bush and barked. I threw a pebble at the dog, hitting him in the hind leg. The dog remained vigilant and continued to bark at Primo's face that must have blinked in horror as it saw, for a final split second, the sight of this mongrel.

The *parang*, sharp as a scimitar, edged with Primo's blood, was re-placed in the cousin's belt.

Several villagers hauled the body onto a large plank and dragged it away to an arid field. I went with them. Due to the drought, our shovels bit with difficulty into the dry earth. The digging took an hour. Flies and dogs quickly congregated. No person wished to be there. After the body had been tossed in and the grave refilled, the other men left. I marked the grave with two sticks tied together into a cross. There is an unwholesome-ness to burying a decapitated corpse. It was as if one were burying a dog and not a human being. Alone, I mumbled a few words, what I recollected from the Lord's Prayer.

When I arrived back in the village, Wang ran up to me. "Where is he?" he asked feebly.

Somehow he had received word of Primo's execution. News like that was hard to conceal in a village starved for gossip.

I shrugged. "I don't know," I said.

Usually there was the humdrum existence of everyday life, the farmers going into the field, the children playing in the roads, the women working, cooking, the games of evening checkers, and the sound of automatic weapons at night and heard infrequently during the daytime. I had grown used to this existence and must confess that I had become fond of the lifestyle, the ease of this dull and daily routine, and could have found reasonable contentment if not for Thompson.

"Tell me," Wang begged.

I was surprised by his distress. He appeared ready to keel over.

"In the east field," I finally said. "We buried him there."

I withheld the fact we hadn't been able to locate Primo's head. The mongrel, pissed for having a stone heaved at him, had growled at me, snapped up Primo's head, and run off. It was my sole act of kindness toward Wang. Dejected, he left.

Melinda walked up to me and said, "Sam, Oung Yi's inside her hut. She needs to be cleaned up. Will you help her?"

I glanced at the hut's doorway.

"No. Better it's a woman."

I had the sudden intuition Yi had known all along I had been watching her bathe, cowering in the woods, bewitched by her deformity and beauty.

"The village women won't help because of the rape," Melinda explained. "She's shamed by it. And I don't know why she won't let me. I offered. But she'll let you. She didn't tell me that. It's just a guess. I think she loves you."

"I can't," I said.

"Please, darling. She needs your help."

Melinda went to the hut's doorway and spoke briefly to Oung Yi. Then she marched over the bridge toward Thompson's compound. I went to Oung Yi's hut, knocked on a wooden slat, and announced myself. For a moment, I hesitated after she said to come in. A buried emotion within me, my desire for her, perhaps, resisted the image I had constructed. I didn't want to see Oung Yi in bed, helpless. I felt disheartened as I entered.

Inside, she sat in a chair, an unlit lantern beside her. Her fingers held a spool of yarn but no needle, and the colorful cloth, the foot-square beginnings of a blanket, rested on her ankle. She raised a hand and waved rather grandly.

I bent my face near hers. "What can I do?" I asked in a quiet voice.

Her head lowered. "I don't need help," she answered.

I laid a hand on her dirty fingers and her bloodied palm.

"Let's go to the river. Let's clean you up."

"Yes," she said. "I am dirty."

Oung Yi placed the spool on the table. I went to the mat to retrieve her artificial limb, but she objected, saying, "It hurts."

Like I had with the old man from Preah Vihear, I lifted her up, so light she was, it was as if she, too, were vanishing before my eyes, and carried her in my arms. On the path, she spoke to a passing villager who avoided her gaze. Just over the rise I stumbled on a stone, and Oung Yi seized my neck more tightly. The stump shifted in my arms, and the surprisingly hard muscle pressed firmly into her other leg.

At the river, I could do no more than bathe her as if she were my child. Her outer clothes, except for the sarong she wore, lay across a boulder. I swabbed her arms and a wide scrape that ran from her throat and slanted diagonally across her chest. I washed behind her ears, along her neck, washing with firm, gentle strokes, moving the bar of soap in circles, massaging the tense shoulder muscles. Next I held the stump on my thigh, ran my thumb over the dark sutured skin and soaped the stump, cleansing it with handfuls of river water. I cleaned her ankle, her foot, and the five supple toes. Leaning closer, I lathered the few hairs beneath her arms, and briefly turned my back as she washed her breasts and below.

She never said a word. Her breathing was as mute as her artificial limb. She shut her eyes, and with my soapy hands I touched her face, brushing with delicate strokes the soft ovals of her eyes, her sepia lips, and her handsome jaw line. I admit I was tempted to kiss her, but not out of passion. I wanted her forgiveness for having failed to prevent the attack.

"You'll leave with Melinda and me," I said.

She remained silent, and I sensed her weakening resistance to the idea.

With newfound conviction, I pulled her toward me so that her chin rested on my shoulder and scrubbed her lower back, veined with dirt and tiny scratches. I was sockless, shoeless, and had rolled my pants above me knees. It was to no avail. The water surged around me. I settled waist deep into the river, and washed her wrists and hands, the callused palms and fingers that did Thompson's bidding. The image pressed deeper into my thoughts, our exit from this land.

CHAPTER 24

⁂

DARKNESS DESCENDED AND I returned Oung Yi to her hut, her mat, and pulled the blanket over her body.

"There are devils," she said before I exited. "I know you see them."

"Yes," I said. "They are people with black hearts. But sleep. No one will harm you tonight."

"Take Melinda away from here. Her mother is dead. No one can bring back the dead. Memories can't bring them back." It was as if she were speaking to her Lord Buddha. "When I was young, my father hurt me down here. I know how wrong that is, and I can never forgive him or myself. Take my sister away from here. Protect her. Promise me."

I did. That evening, I sat outside my hut wrapped in a blanket. My body trembled from a cool mountain breeze. Tomorrow, I told myself, Melinda and I will leave. Thompson's control over her would finally cease.

As a bird passed across the face of the moon, a figure, Oung Yi, I believed, walked along the road. Holding a lantern, she hobbled over the bridge. It was late for her to make the journey to Thompson's compound, and I wondered which demon possessed her to go at night to his hut.

Somewhere in the jungle darkness a twig snapped. I shivered. In Thompson's compound, Oung Yi's lit lantern had vanished, and the image of Thompson assaulting her body filled my thoughts. I cast off the blanket, put on my sandals, and walked toward the narrow bridge. The smell of wood smoke drifted from Thompson's compound, and the jungle noises seemed non-existent. Passing a wooden stanchion carved into a dragon's head, I walked cautiously over the bridge and lingered on the other side. Suddenly someone shouted in Khmer, and

I slunk against one of the huts, listening to the sound of approaching footsteps. The person was in a hurry. I heard the rapid breaths of the stranger and peeked around the corner of the hut. It was Oung Yi. For a moment, as she went over the rickety bridge, it appeared she might misstep and fall into the river below. I was prepared to come to her aid, but she guided herself expertly, the affliction in her hip socket where the artificial limb met bone, no doubt, painful. She stopped on the far side of the bridge and faced me. Her willowy shape was partially eaten away by the darkness. I stepped onto the road and half expected her to call my name, but she turned and walked off.

In the main compound I heard music, xylophones and gongs. The tranquil sound was a musical offering to the good spirits. I halted, trying to discern from which hut the sound emanated. A moment passed and the music stopped.

Moving forward, I worked my flashlight on and off at random intervals, so as not to stumble or scare a peasant. At one junction, I spotted two goats, one mounted on the other, and in a small garden a tiny bronze Buddha.

At Thompson's hut, the shutter was partway down. A candle burned in his hut, emitting a soft light. I tested the door. It was unlatched, and I went in. There was no sign of the cockatoo; his perch was empty. The room seemed larger in the night, and I smelled a faint, sweet odor like that of scented soap. I stepped forward. My plan was ordained. Nothing could disrupt it. I would threaten Thompson with the knife I had stolen from Oung Yi's room, the one she used in the kitchen for skinning and chopping. He would confess his errors and tell Melinda the truth about her mother. Finally, we would be free of him.

I removed the knife from my belt and held it in my right hand. Thompson lay on his bed, his white hair, long and loose, covering an ear and a section of his leathery neck where I would draw the knife blade. His eyes were closed, his knees raised to belt level. He appeared to be asleep. I wanted to shake Thompson, have him view the knife and profoundly realize his blunder in underestimating me.

I reached for his shoulder. His shirt was damp. From somewhere inside the hut, a woman said, "Don't. You can't wake him."

I withdrew my hand and spun toward the voice.

"Melinda?" I whispered.

She sat in a chair, in a dark corner, a few feet from the bed.

"What's going on?"

"I hit him," she said. "Maybe I killed him."

She rose and walked toward me. I couldn't help but notice how exceptionally small she looked, like a thinning shadow on a wall. She stood beside me.

"Nothing matters anymore," she said.

"Tell me what happened."

"He assaulted Oung Yi."

I moved toward the body and pulled hard on the shoulder, for I had to verify this news. He tumbled over with a grunt. His chest heaved, his mouth opened, and I stared at the stained teeth and black tongue. Slowly his eyes widened. He blinked, and I stumbled backward as Thompson sat up and dropped his legs over the edge of the bed.

"Daughter," he said in a hoarse voice. "What have you done?"

"Don't talk to him," Melinda said, fiercely.

"I don't understand."

"I told you already. He was with Oung Yi. A while ago I left him to bathe at the river. And when I came back, he was forcing himself on her."

"I can't make love, Daughter. What you witnessed wasn't what you think."

"She's my sister. How could you do such a thing?"

Thompson shook his head. "She often comforts me at night. You should have informed me you were returning."

"Wang told me you were sleeping with her, but I didn't believe him."

"He'll say anything for money. He's disappointed I haven't been more generous. Perhaps your lover bribed him to say those things to you?"

Melinda murmured the word *lover* as if confused by its meaning.

I lit the bedside lamp. Thompson's cheek, bluish-black in the light, had a two-inch shallow cut. Melinda must have given him a right cross.

"Did you tell Sam about us?" Thompson asked. "I want you to tell him now how each day you pretended to be your mother. I let you act out your fantasy. You wanted to be her. I showed you her things, and you wore your mother's clothes, her jewelry. I told you stories, described to you what she looked like, her face, her body. The way she smelled, and the way her skin felt." He held out his hands, as if in supplication, and looked at me. "How do you describe that? The way a woman feels in your arms, against your body. The way a woman can suffer, the way an old man can. I'm eighty-three, but I don't forget. Melinda lay beside me. She's my daughter, and she pretended to be my wife. What's the harm in a little game? She's small, you know. I don't see how she ever became a mother."

I raised the knife, the curved blade black and solemn. The knife had weight; the handle must have been made of stone. I had the will to do it: direct, simple, focused. I thought of nothing else but the swift movement of my arm accelerating as the knife sliced skin and smashed bone and the lush life ending for this old man.

"No," Melinda cried. "Say whatever you like to him, but don't hurt him. Say what's on your mind. I give you that much."

"Damn your philosophy, Thompson. I don't give a rat's ass about your goodness anymore. I don't care what you know concerning Melinda's mother. You're a bastard. And we're through with you."

My fingers opened. The knife dropped from my hand and landed with a thump on the ground. Melinda sat down in the chair, her hands in her lap.

"What is it you want to tell me?" Melinda asked. "Do you want to call me names, Sam? You can. Call me fool. Tramp. A lousy mother, and a lousy friend. I've used them all, said them to myself. Anything to make you feel better. That's what we both want, to make you happy." She scratched at her throat. "So often I'm scared of being left alone, when it's I who leave everyone I love. Even you. Now tell me, what will make you feel good?

Do you want me? Yes, you can have me, but just don't touch me. I know, I know that sounds crazy."

"Stop it," I said.

In the distance, I heard gunfire.

"What he said is true, Sam. But I never slept with him. I pretended like he said. I wanted to be loved by her, by my mother. I thought if I could be like my mother I'd know why she left me, if she loved me. How much she loved me. And I know it was a childish game, and games are for children, but I was alone. Even with you I'm alone."

"And did you see your mother more clearly?" I asked.

"No."

"I wish it had worked."

"Really?"

"Of course."

I refastened two buttons on her blouse. Thompson began to rise, but I pushed him down.

"Now tell the truth, old man. Did you ever know Melinda's mother? Is Oung Yi her real sister? No more lies."

Thompson sat up and grinned. The skunk thought he was home free.

"Does it matter?" he asked.

"Damn straight," I told him. "To her and to me."

"You think I've had it easy, don't you? In 1968 the Cambodians abducted me. Yes, I did engineer my own kidnapping. It surprised me, though, the rumor mill it created, and the interest. The great mystery of Jim Thompson's disappearance. The newspapers, the media, they all devoured the report. The attention stunned me. But I had to do it. Life in Bangkok was dismal. In Cambodia, I was going to be their symbol of virility and power. I loved the people. In fact, I thought I was a hero to these people, an icon they would honor and protect. I even married one of their own. My first wife was Cambodian. Yi's mother. A beautiful child. I can't begin to express her devotion. Sorry, Daughter. Oung Yi is not your full-blood sister, but your half-sister. I am your father. But things in

Cambodia changed quickly. Due to the 1970s famine and the rise of the Khmer Rouge regime, I lost everything.

"I remember the night the Khmer Rouge entered my village and tied us up with rope. My wife and I. Oung Yi's mother. She was so loyal. A gentle Buddhist. They had caught her stealing food. I was sick. We were both starving. *'Learn your lesson'* they said. We and three Khmer soldiers sat near a small fire. A skillet cooked over the flames. One of the soldiers took a knife and cut my wife's liver out of her body and tossed it on the hot skillet. She watched and I watched as her liver jumped up and down in the skillet. Then she died. They wouldn't kill me. I was still of some use to them: propaganda, ransom, prestige. I'm not quite sure."

"Another phony story," I said.

"Is it true?" Melinda asked.

Thompson nodded.

"And Oung Yi," I said, feeling sorrow for Oung Yi's mother. "Tonight, what did you do to her?"

For a passing second I was prepared to strike him down with my hands for her sake and for her mother's.

"You raped her," Melinda said.

"She comforts me."

"Your daughter."

"She's my child. I'm impotent. I couldn't harm her."

"Damn you, Father," Melinda said.

"That's good. You feel better. Now give me a kiss."

He opened his arms, but Melinda remained seated.

I nudged his shoulder. "Now the truth. Are you really Melinda's father?"

"All the stories I told her are true."

Melinda rose. She leaned forward and kissed him on the forehead, a kiss so slight and imperceptible in its contact I was sure she had not touched him. Nonetheless, I stared, enviously. Even this gesture, or so it seemed, was one of love.

I asked again, quietly this time, almost respectfully, if he was indeed Melinda's father. He remained silent. A breeze shook the door. I cupped the candle. Outside, beyond the window, I imagined Melinda's mother lurked, wanting to retrieve her daughter from harm.

"Tell me the truth," I demanded.

He looked at Melinda. It was as if the kiss had cleared his mind.

"I was living in Bangkok and was famous in a small way, as you well know. One day I met this Chinese woman. Your mother. The likeness, you'll have to admit, is striking." He snapped his hand beside his ear, as if brushing aside a mosquito. "I wanted to hide this fact from you, but if it's the truth you want here it is. I met your mother in a Bangkok bar where she danced. I paid the bar, and she came home with me. That night she told me her story, where she came from, the poverty of her province, the death of her parents. I gave her extra money in the morning, so she could leave the bar. A year later she came to me with this child in her arms, claiming the child was ours. Of course it wasn't. We'd never consummated. I had been woefully drunk that night. And you were far too beautiful to have been mine."

"But I have your nose and ears," Melinda protested. "Elephant ears just like yours. And you said my breasts were like hers."

"Let's go," I said.

"Is my mother alive?"

"She died of dysentery," Thompson answered. "Her body shriveled up like a pea. Yes, Wang brought other Chinese women here thinking he could trick me into believing they were your mother, so he could get my gold. But I knew she was dead."

"Where is she buried?" Melinda asked.

His chin lowered. "Bangkok. She was cremated. She's in my house. Her ashes are in one of the antique urns from ancient Thailand that tourists pass each day, on a shelf in the armoire."

"A trophy," I murmured.

"She died in my arms," said Thompson.

"Then she lived with you, Father," Melinda said.

"You're clever, entrapping an old man like that. All right. Here's the truth if you want it so badly, if you think it will make a difference. I had wanted to protect you. Oh child, you're so innocent to believe such words can help. Yes, you are my daughter. I took your mother away from whoring and installed her in my kitchen as a cook and my lover. Though she cheated on me. She denied it, but she slept with other men. I could smell it on her, other men's sweat, spit, and their sperm. Sometimes she had bruises on her hips, her knees, and elbows. Once I caught her reading the Kama Sutra in a closet with a candle. She said it was so she could be a better lover to me. It was to be a surprise, her new-fangled ways of making love. But I knew it was for her lovers. So I kicked her out, booted you as well into the street. I was wrong, Daughter. Callused to love. I'd had the dengue fever for so long and was delirious. Months later she came back. It was monsoon season. The rains had come. Floods destroyed villages. Cholera bubbled on the ground, rode in the air. Infection. Disease. The few Catholics spoke of pestilence. A mean season that year.

"Your mother was standing outside my house. She was ill. Her eyes were yellow, her skin shriveled. I remember when I traced my fingers along her temple her hair came off in my hand. It had always been thick, but now it was cancerously thin. She weighed thirty kilos. Maybe less. But you were healthy, crying, banging your tiny fists on your mother's breast. She didn't ask for help, but just stood shivering in the rain. I wish you could have seen her at that moment. She looked like some kind of angel. I can't forget. She's locked inside here." He tapped his head. "Well, I took her in, got her to bed, and called the doctor. She didn't die that night. But she never again spoke a single word to me and refused to forgive me. She became my housekeeper, but her health didn't return. She died four years later. Influenza, I think. Another bad season. She told nobody. She must have been ill for days. One day she took to bed and hours later she was gone without a word. So like her. A selfish woman to the end. She had no sense of responsibility. After all, she left me to take care of you.

"She died a week before I was to leave Thailand. My kidnapping had been all arranged. I couldn't take you with me. I apologize. Someone told me of a good orphanage in Hong Kong and relatives you had living there. It was for the best. In those days I wasn't a father. I saw you maybe once a week when I'd descend the stairs to your mother's bedroom for an hour or two. Child, there's no greater grief than the silence of lovemaking. I had to be with her now and again. She was a narcotic for me. It was always late night, and you slept heavily. I was a ghost to you. That's why you have no memory of me.

Thompson rocked forward. "Your mother was a whore to the last. It pains me even now to acknowledge it. The dear, sweet thing. You should have seen all the letters of regret at her passing. The men that sent flowers. The passionate verse written to her character, her charm. Several men wept openly at the funeral. And you, Daughter, reawakened her for me. I thank you and curse you. Your mother was so beautiful in her diminutive way. We were perfect lovers. But she could eat a man's soul. I was a weakling to her passions, and a slave to my own. Thankfully her death allowed me to escape unhindered, or so I thought. Yet, I couldn't rid you from my mind. For years, I recalled everything about you, dreamed of your face and voice, imagined the woman you'd become. You haunted me. Fortunately, I had Wang doing my errands. Even back in Thailand, Wang worked for me and kept tabs on you. He's a clever dog. He tracked me up here after I disappeared."

"You can't believe a word," I said.

Melinda's fingers circled my arm, gripping my bicep. Her bony shoulder leaned into mine, and I smelled her breath, which I drank up like a love potion.

"So, Wang found me by chance?" Melinda asked.

"No. Our amiable Buddha. His light guided Wang. And your letters, of course."

The lantern fluttered in a strange breeze, and I said, "We need to close the shutter."

"Hush, Sam." I watched her tongue, lithe like a lizard's, wet her lips. "Jim," she said. "You look tired." She bent down and retrieved the knife from the floor. "Don't ever touch my sister again."

"Your sister knows I'd never harm her." Thompson glared at me. "Don't forget, you promised to take her away from here. Do that. Do that one good thing."

Melinda stepped toward the door. "Let's go, Sam. I don't belong here anymore."

We left the little hut. The door creaked as it closed. On the road to the village, our shadows cast huge shapes on the hard earth. It was as if we were from a different race, Melinda and I, not insect or animal or human, but beings that moved between flesh and air.

Before I could inquire about her condition, Melinda said, "It doesn't matter where my mother is. I know what you're thinking. That her ashes aren't in that urn locked away in his house. She did her best, didn't she? That's what counts. She protected me. She made the best of her life, of what she had and who she was. I know he killed her in his own way, and I know he shunned the one thing that matters in this life. The love of a man and the love of a woman. I feel sorry for him."

She took hold of my hand and squeezed my fingers. The palm of her hand was hot and sweaty, and when she kissed my mouth I thought I felt the caress of another woman, one who had tried her best in an unforgiving world and had failed to find the home she desired. Melinda's body slackened, and her nose pressed my cheek.

As we walked, her face looked as smooth as always, undamaged yet saddened, as if the tiny muscles below the skin had wept, and it frightened me a little to see such strength in the woman I loved.

Near the bridge, a figure half hidden alongside a hut motioned to me. I slowed. Melinda ambled ahead. Only when she stepped foot on the bridge did she realize my absence. She glanced at me, I waved her on, and she continued to the village. Backtracking several meters, I returned to the area where I had seen the figure.

"Oung Yi," I said faintly, "where are you?"

"I want the gold," a voice called out.

"Wang, is that you?"

He came forward, materializing from the blackness.

"You look surprised," Wang said.

"I thought you were someone else."

"Who?"

"Never mind."

"Primo shouldn't have harmed Oung Yi," he admitted with a shrug. "He shouldn't have touched her no matter how attractive she is. I think her affliction enticed him, and her pretty face. She looks so much like our honey, Melinda."

As I moved to leave, he cuffed my wrist. With a jerk, I pulled my hand free.

"Did you see Thompson?" Wang asked.

"I did."

"Where has he hidden the money?" Wang asked in a heated tone. "Did he tell you?"

The land had darkened as a few clouds covered the moon.

"Forget the money. He'll tell no one."

"You bastard. He trusts you and our girl. What did you do to ruin everything?"

"He told us about Melinda's mother."

"Maybe he told your girl about the money's location. Let's find her. She'll talk. A little push in the right direction and she'll tell us where the boodle is."

I seized his throat with my hands and felt the cords and glands, the fat and cartilage. I was tempted to bang his face into the nearby hut. But after a few moments I released him.

He coughed. The clouds passed, exhibiting a river of moonlight.

"Merlin, you always had a screw loose." He spat on the ground, massaging his throat. "Now back to important matters, my boy."

"Hit the road," I said.

Wang moved up alongside me. "You coward, you've blown my life's work. I'm not going to die in these hills. You're responsible for my nephew's death."

Without warning, Wang shoved me in the shoulder, a jolt that sent me stumbling backward toward the jungle. Before I could fully regain my balance, he ran at me, bent at the waist, both arms outright. Surprisingly nimble-footed, he struck me forcefully in the hip. My feet slipped on the dry dirt and I fell, seizing Wang's shirtsleeve and dragging him with me. We rolled down a short slope over vines, small stones, and burnt embers. Broken branches pinched my belly and legs. Wang, in tune with my momentum, bounced on my chest, and I felt his nose crunch against my chin. We came to rest amid a mass of palm fronds.

I rose to my feet. I had little need for Wang, his treasure, or the dilapidated dream he offered Melinda.

"You know what I want," Wang said, pulling out his handkerchief. I had given him a bloody nose.

"Start digging," I told him. "The treasure's bound to be buried nearby."

Wang's eyes swept the terrain. "Are you serious?" he asked, dabbing his nose with the handkerchief.

"Yes. Why not? Thompson wouldn't keep his loot in his hut."

Wang grimaced and came to his feet. "I think you're right. Listen, if you help me a little more I'll take you to Melinda's mother. She's still alive."

"So long, Wang."

I climbed the hill as Wang struggled after me. The night air was pristine, and as I strode toward the bridge I noted a light from my hut.

"Come back here, Merlin."

I glanced over my shoulder. He had followed me a few yards down the road and stopped. He had both fists in the air, the bloody handkerchief tucked into the top of his shirt. As I walked, the darkness seemed to eat away at his body.

"My nephew's dead," he hollered. "My life's work, being an errand boy for that old goat, and for what? Answer me. For what?"

What regret I had then I don't recall. But as I approached the bridge I realized Melinda had matured in these last few weeks, and by doing so she would soon see me for the man I was: in need like she had been, a nonviolent man in a crazed world. I never disclosed this to her, and to this day I wish I had told her of my fear and the true nature of my character.

CHAPTER 25

AFTER CROSSING THE bridge, instead of taking the road to my hut, I walked toward Oung Yi's hut. I knocked, heard a quiet response, and entered.

A lantern was lit on a round table, and she sat in a chair, cradling her right arm. A cloth had been tied around her right hand, and I noted streaks of blood on her fingers.

"What happened?" I asked, pulling a chair next to hers. "Let me see your hand."

The cloth, wet with blood, was sticky. Carefully I unwrapped the cloth, placing my fingertips on the underside of her wrist for support.

"Is it bad?" she asked.

"It's only a scratch."

A small-caliber bullet, or so it appeared, had nicked the fatty part of her hand. It may have been a ricochet or a wildly fired shot from one of the Khmer soldiers. The blood flow was minimal; a small chunk of her palm was missing. I put my handkerchief in her lap and rested her hand on top of it.

"I have to clean the wound."

"There are some medicines in the kitchen cabinet," Oung Yi said.

I went into the kitchen, lit the stove, and placed a pot on the metal burner. Quickly the water came to a boil, and I hauled the pot and the medicines into the room. I cleaned the wound and the blood on her hand with the water. Her medicine kit held fresh gauze pads, plastic stitches, Betadine, and tape. The Betadine cauterized the wound, and after I applied the plastic stitches and the final strip of tape, securing the gauze pad to her hand, I put everything back into the medicine kit.

"You'll have to get some antibiotic in case of infection. There's a doctor in the village of Kompong Thom, I think. I know the village is many miles away, but it's important."

"You are very kind. How can I thank you?"

"Come with me and Melinda. Tomorrow we leave. Live with us in Hong Kong."

Oung Yi pulled the wounded hand into her mid-section. "This is my home," she said. "I would be lost anywhere else. Be happy in your life. I will think of you always as my friend."

She began to unfasten her wooden limb. I moved to help her, but she pushed my hand away. With her left hand beneath the skirt, I heard the release of Velcro and straps, and Oung Yi's sigh of relief as she pulled the object free and leaned it against the chair.

"I wonder," she said, "if the drought will end soon. The fields are dry, and if we don't get rain the rice will die. I like the smell of rain in the rice fields." She massaged the stump. "I hear there is a wheelchair shop in the village of Banteay. I can work there and make money, though Jesuits run it. I don't want my village to starve. These people are my friends. I have family nearby. They're farmers with six buffaloes, and without the rain there will be sickness and starvation. You can't stay where you do not belong."

Her little face held a dignity that made me uncomfortable. For days, I had carried the jewels in my pocket, the one's I had stuffed into my shaving razor in Bangkok, in case Melinda and I needed to leave spur of the moment. I removed the jewels from my pocket, opened the small purse, and spilled them onto her lap. She fingered a couple, unsure of their nature.

"Diamonds and rubies," I said. "They'll help you, your family, and the village."

"There are others," she said, pressing them into her lap, "who need the Rolls Royce of leg. Thank you for this."

She gathered the jewels off her skirt, the small stones glinting now and again in the lamplight, appearing like drops of river water in her brown hand. When she had them all, she held out her half-closed fist and let them fall, pouring from her fingers into my hand. They felt cold in my palm, and once I had them all, I opened my fingers and let the jewels shower back onto Oung Yi's black skirt. She put the jewels in a pink handkerchief and tied a knot around them.

I asked her, "Are you tired?" She nodded. "Do you need help to get to bed?"

"Yes."

I picked her up, placed her on the straw-woven mattress, and she pulled the thin blanket up to her waist.

"Can you stay with me until I fall asleep? I sense there are demons out tonight."

"They're gone," I said. "There's no need to be afraid."

I cannot begin to explain my exhaustion or my need to be beside her. It seems unfathomable that I wanted this woman when Melinda waited in our hut for my return. For a few minutes, I told myself, I would comply with Oung Yi's request. Perhaps my presence would dissuade the demons she spoke about from entering her hut. The fact is, I wanted the simplicity and comfort that Oung Yi represented. I wanted to lay beside someone with whom there was no past or future, and I wanted to temporarily escape the events that for weeks had torn at me.

She tucked the blanket beneath her body, and I turned off the lantern. Stretching out beside her, the mat groaned beneath our weight. My head rested on the single long pillow. I breathed deeply, expecting my body to relax, my muscles to fall into a peaceful state.

"How do you feel, Sam?"

"Fine."

I could not unwind. For the first time in a long while I knew where I belonged, and it wasn't here with this kind woman. I listened to the dark. The jungle noise, the insects and animals, emitted a soft murmur. In the hut, Oung Yi's breathing was barely audible. She remained perfectly still, and I could smell her fragrant hair and imagined the tenderness of her mouth if kissed, her need to be loved. I sat up, resting my arms in my lap.

"Do you have to go?" Oung Yi asked.

"Yes. I'm sorry."

"You will be in my prayers."

I walked the winding path through the village to the hut with the burning lantern, entered, and saw Melinda asleep on the straw mat. I lowered the lantern's flame and sat in a chair. She lay on her back, her hands on her stomach, the lantern's glow bathing her face in a reddish hue. I believed her emotional wounds would heal in time, and the conflict that had absorbed her for most of her life would slacken and eventually disappear. She would mature into the woman she was destined to become, and she would be united with her son. These things I believed with certainty. In my life, I had known no one with her resolve, and her understanding that life was not a path of rules, but was one of trials. And it is only by the course of those trials that a person can determine their future. I lowered the lantern flame until the wick failed and slid beside Melinda on the straw mat.

CHAPTER 26

THE FOLLOWING MORNING a stiff wind blew. Than, Melinda, and I marched out of the village and onto a rice plateau, where the lean rice stalks arched against the sapphire sky.

We went southward, skirting the Tonle Sap River, and took the road that led to Phnom Penh. The trek took three days. We carried drinking water and rice, walking many miles in extreme heat, though we always rested during the midday. At night, we slept in secluded villages, safe from the Khmer Rouge.

Late one morning, we stopped on the outskirts of the capital, a few kilometers from the old stadium, now closed, and the destroyed Chruoy Changvar Bridge. Than would go no farther. Before we left him, Melinda handed him her gold hoop earrings, which she had plucked from her earlobes. Than pressed his hands together below his chin, hooted with delight, and placed the gold hoops on his fingers. He waved, and he shooed us down the road.

In Phnom Penh, Melinda and I stayed overnight at the Hotel Cambodiana. While Melinda slept, I made arrangements for departure. Our flight was late evening the following day. The next morning, under Melinda's urging, we rented a Jeep with a driver, Bundrith, and drove to the killing fields, approximately fifteen kilometers outside the capital.

"In order to survive," she said," we need to remember history."

The city road was rutted and half paved. We passed the congested open market with its overburdened straw baskets of rice, the fresh fish and vegetables laid out on shaded wooden tables. On sidewalks, in bright sunlight, women sawed huge blocks of ice. Later, traveling south on Monrieth

Boulevard, I observed a barber cutting hair, the chair positioned beneath a lamppost, the man's face reflected in a mirror hung on a wrought-iron fence. Nearby, a makeshift bicycle repair shop had been set up, the mechanic's tools spread on the asphalt. Melinda nudged my arm. A barefoot boy hurried along the sidewalk holding a brick of ice secured by a string, his hand clutching the string like a leash.

With a smile, Bundrith hit the Jeep's brake, swung left into the next lane, facing oncoming motorbikes, cyclos, and bicycles. He honked as several motorbikes swerved around us. By instinct, he accelerated, passed an easy-going cyclo on our right, and pulled back into the proper lane.

Outside of Phnom Penh the pavement turned into a slender dirt road, bordered by rice paddies. We crossed two shaky wooden bridges at five miles per hour. Skinny water buffaloes were tethered to trees, and wooden stands for Coke and Tiger beer lined the roadway.

We turned onto a dirt path and parked. After we walked through the open gate, Bundrith pointed past the tall monument on our left toward the notorious fields a few meters ahead. In the shade of a palm tree, two boys manned a portable Coca Cola stand.

I stopped a meter before the expansive field. The earth was parched and overgrown with weeds and tufts of coarse grass. It hadn't always been this way. I imagined this ground a decade ago, barren, chock full of skeletons. Somehow, flora had returned. I breathed through one nostril and out the other like a good Buddhist. I counted my breaths.

Melinda roamed into the field. There were several deep pits or ditches, some dry, others partially filled with a murky, greenish water, where the skeletal remains from the mass graves had been excavated. A barbed wire fence circled a larger field, preventing trespass. The excavation had ceased at this point. Bundrith pointed at the plaques above the holes that listed the found dead. *Mass Grave of 166 Victims Without Heads.*

Melinda, holding her instamatic camera, patrolled the pits. She stopped, crouched, and moved her hand along the ground.

"I've found a bone," she called out. "I can't believe it. There are so many. It's been years since the killings. Look, Sam."

She got down on one knee, camera in hand, the viewfinder plugged against her eye, and snapped a photo of the bones. With her boot toe, she touched a bone the size of a forearm that protruded from one of the pits. Digging into the ground with her fingers, she picked up a small bow-shaped bone, white as an eggshell. Perhaps it had been a finger or part of a foot. She blew off the dirt. After a minute, her hand lowered, and the bone rolled off her fingers and fell to the ground. A white butterfly circled above her shoulder. Not far off, a rooster crowed in the humid air.

Feeling dizzy, I walked toward the shaded monument. The Kampuchean government had erected a glass and concrete monument to the victims of these killing fields. I climbed up the steps toward the large glass door. Once inside, I pressed my back to the smooth granite wall and relished the cooler air. Less than a yard in front of me was a two-tiered glass partition. Imprisoned behind the glass were floors of human skulls, hundreds of them, layered one on top of the other, many with teeth still in place. Tattered clothes lay in a pile beneath the first tier. The skulls were labeled and sectioned off according to age: 10- to 14-year olds, 20- to 40-year olds, 50- to 60-year old Kampucheans, and a section for Europeans. With my back to the wall, I circled the entombed skulls.

Halfway around, I reached out and, with a single fingertip, touched the glass which held the skulls. I expected nothing, neither heat nor cold, but the glass was amazingly warm, like a windowpane in a suburban home on a spring day.

I exited in a strange, exalted panic, donned my sunglasses and stood beneath the shade of a towering Kray Sor tree.

Melinda returned, brushing her dirty hands on her pants. "This place gives me the creeps," she said. She shifted her camera. "Smile, Sam," she said and shot a picture of me. "You look like a playboy."

Before we departed I excused myself, walked off, ducked behind some brush, and vomited. My stomach was nearly empty, but it didn't matter. Melinda found me, bent at the waist, holding onto a tree trunk.

"Go away," I said.

"What's wrong? You sick?"

"Go away, please."

She put her hand on my shoulder. It was as if I were falling and the ground beneath me had changed into a marsh of quicksand.

"You're cold. Are you all right?"

I remained silent and shivering. She reached for me, those warm, brown-skinned hands that sought me out wherever I was, took hold of my face and gently lifted me up, inch by inch, until I stood erect. Her hot breath touched my cheek, and the cool blue sky appeared behind her head. Her black hair was tied back with a colored ribbon, pulled taut against her skull with a few wild strands frizzed from the high humidity, and the sunlight, pale as sheer silk, fell across her brow.

I couldn't find the proper words. I tried, but as one after the other lit upon my tongue, they vanished. *Don't ever leave me*, I thought. I leaned against her. Her hand stroked my forehead.

"Must be the water," I said at last. "I drank from the tap this morning."

"You know better than that."

We waited in the windless air, the sunlight like cut glass inches from our feet. It wasn't the skulls or tattered clothes that made me vomit. The reason was simple, but I wouldn't admit it to myself. It was my own fear of death. But that, too, was a lie. Just as I had witnessed the bone roll off Melinda's hand, I recalled Oung Yi's stump in my hands at the riverbed. I had been surprised at the partial leg's suppleness. I had felt the edge of the bone beneath the skin. And, as Melinda and I stood in the shade, I knew I had abandoned Yi in a way that would be impossible to forget.

CHAPTER 27

A FEW HOURS before our departure from Phnom Penh to Bangkok, Melinda sat on the bed's white sheets, her clothes piled on the floor. The shutters were fastened. A dampness settled in the air and on her body that made the room seem smaller, more secretive. She removed the purple ribbon from her hair. I undressed, drank a glass of distilled water, went toward her and stood beside the bed. First she took my penis in her mouth, and when she felt I was ripe, she said, "With your mouth, please." I knelt down, and parted her legs and the fragrant hairs below her abdomen, opening her with my fingers, tasting the center of her as she stretched backward onto the bed.

Her moistness seeped into my mouth, onto my tongue, down my chin. She came in small, almost imperceptible shudders.

"You're going to leave me," she said, as I left her sex and kissed her flat belly. "You're going to forget me, but it's all right."

"Never," I said.

I was inside her now, her ankles looped over mine. She kissed me deeply over and over again, holding me firmly by the nape of my neck. I began to roll so that we could lie side by side, but she resisted, and said, "Just like this. I want it this way, and stay in me afterward. Don't leave me."

"I want to marry you," I said.

"Yes, I want to marry you, too."

I brushed her lips with my finger, and she whispered my name. Her skin was sticky, and I kissed her neck, the sweat salty on my tongue.

Her fingers touched the hair of my groin, and I said to her, "Say it again, my name."

Instead, her mouth reared upward, and she kissed and bit until my lip ached. I came and shrunk inside her. We lay locked together, just as Melinda wished. Then she rolled onto her side, reached down, and held me in her hand.

"I like when you're soft," she said, "and I make you hard."

I closed my eyes. We were stranded, Melinda and I, and the bed was a raft and Cambodia our sea. I slept and dreamed and in the dream Melinda and I were in a raft. The sea was red, and bodies floated to the water's surface. There were hundreds of bodies, and I felt ashamed, for I did nothing. I didn't close their eyes or ask if they needed help. Shall I deliver a message to your family? Is there an errand you need performed? Come on, get it off your chest. I withdrew to the center of the raft. When I saw the armless Khmer soldier girl, I reached for her, but she kicked away from me, a flutter kick that disturbed the water's placid surface. She was still angry, I believed, by my final parting gesture at Preah Vihear. "Sam," Melinda said, and I looked at her on the other side of the raft and saw she was clothed in an electric-blue dress.

I awoke to the smell of jasmine.

"Wake up, darling," Melinda said, fresh from a shower. "I want you again."

I obeyed and grew hard as she caressed me. Touching her belly, and the short black satiny hairs on her thigh, I heard a sharp wind slap at the shutters. She swung on top of me and placed me inside her.

"Once more. I want to feel you come inside me again," she said in a most serious voice. "I want to be with you, like this, always."

On the airplane, I sat by the window. Melinda had the aisle seat. The two-engine plane lifted smoothly from Pochentong airport into the cloudless sky, banked left, and climbed to an altitude of 10,000 feet. We ate sandwiches, drank coffee, and kept the pens which had *Bangkok Airways* imprinted on them that the stewardess had distributed. Melinda wore a burgundy shirt, shorts, sneakers, and a white shelled bracelet she had traded a T-shirt for with one of the women from the Thai Palong hill tribe. The beret that Thompson had given her was stored in her travel bag.

I admired the colored beads that dangled like wind chimes from her braided hair. During the plane ride, Melinda spoke with a calculated firmness to her voice, of travel, maps, journeying great distances, and her son. She spoke of mundane matters: tickets, Hong Kong's winter, and the straw peasant hat that had cost her three hundred riels in Phnom Penh.

"I want to put the hat on my wall," she said. "I don't know how I'll carry it without it being damaged. Already two strips are broken."

I had stowed the straw hat below her seat.

An hour into the flight, the plane shuddered, dipped to our left, and dropped several hundred feet. I looked out the window and noted small boats and white crests on the Gulf of Thailand. My ears popped. A groaning sound, like a man sprawled on the street, beaten and bloodied, raced through the plane. The plane pitched downward.

The pilot came on the intercom. He introduced himself; he was Canadian, and our left engine, he informed us, had seized. I looked out the window and could see the propeller and make out each individual silver prop. The plane's wingtips rocked several degrees. Melinda remained silent, her hands, dark as coral, cupped on her knees.

Her skin had broken out in goose flesh. She pulled my sweater, the one I had carried onto the plane in case the air conditioner was too high, over her bare legs.

I touched Melinda's hand, and she gave me a smile, disturbingly peaceful, a smile that said, *We are in Buddha's arms.*

Behind us a man talked boisterously. "My brother went down in one of these crates last year. All twenty passengers dead."

"Shut your mouth," shouted a woman with a British accent.

A stewardess told us to buckle our seatbelts. The plane jolted, the wheels were lowered, and I felt the centrifugal force of decent and motion in my belly.

"We're going to be all right," I said to Melinda.

A green land mass came into view. We passed through cumulus clouds and banked until the Gulf receded and the land sailed beneath the plane. I could distinguish the tops of palm trees, the square plots of rice fields, and tiny objects that resembled water buffaloes. The sunlight shimmered off the field's watered troughs. The approach was simple. We descended, rocking slightly from side to side. The good engine, pressed to its limit, emitted a high whine. There was an odd stillness to the quiet engine, as if we had the capability to fly effortlessly on the wind.

The air strip appeared in front of us. Soon I saw the visible dust of dirt roads, a few natives before the air field leaning on their motorbikes, waving. At palm tree level, a golf course appeared, one immaculate green hole after another, beside the runway.

The wheels touched down and a cheer went up in the cabin. Melinda leaned toward me, her hand on my forearm, and I felt the white Palong shells from the broken string bracelet fall onto the back of my wrist.

CHAPTER 28

"I want to buy one of those ancient bottles with the colored jewels that looks like they hold a genie," Melinda said.

We had gone window shopping during the high hour of the day. Now in the blaze of Bangkok's rush hour, we stood close together on the sidewalk, like two thinly clothed lovers huddled against a winter chill.

Melinda shouted above the roar of traffic on Silom road, "I'll take a *tuc-tuc* back to that antique store on Rama IV road and meet you at the hotel in an hour."

Forget it," I said. "It's broiling. And those so called ancient bottles are a dime a dozen. You can find them at any outdoor bazaar."

"I want one," she insisted.

"They're not worth much."

"That's what you say now, but perhaps there is a genie inside mine." She laughed. "And all your wishes will come true."

"All right," I said, mildly disappointed. "I'll see you at the hotel. Do you have enough money?"

"Oh, sure."

She turned, hailed a *tuc-tuc*, and sped off. The *tuc-tuc* zigzagged between several cars and scooted past a taxi. I lost sight of them when they stalled in traffic near the corner.

I walked slowly in the opposite direction. A girl in a yellow dress sat on a doorstep clipping her toenails. On the next block, rows upon rows of vending stalls crowded the sidewalk. Many vendors reclined on lounge chairs beneath umbrellas, escaping the hot sun. One of the vendors drank a pink liquid with a straw from a plastic bag. Tourists, in shorts and loudly designed short-sleeve shirts, grazed before the stalls, picking at various items: T-shirts, imitation Rolex watches, leather and snake-skin belts, fake designer's pants, and fancy silver lighters.

I was fingering an embroidered vest when I heard the crash of metal and glass. Immediately, I turned and saw a boy running between automobiles, holding a fistful of lottery tickets. Several vendors craned their necks and looked up the road. Soon I found myself moving toward the collision.

After a hundred meters, I saw fruits and vegetables from an overturned motorbike scattered in the road. Traffic had come to a standstill. The driver of the motorbike, an elderly woman, sat crying amid oranges and mangos; her arm had been sliced open, her blouse spattered in blood. The lottery boy, perhaps the old woman's grandson, sat beside her, his hands cupped beneath her wound.

A few yards ahead a *tuc-tuc* had been demolished, flattened like an accordion against a bus. Dazed, passengers exited the bus, gazing at its dented nose, the broken headlights, and the cracked windshield. The *tuc-tuc* driver had been flung sideways and had landed against several people on the sidewalk, knocking them down. He was out cold.

Then I spotted Melinda's handbag in the street. I ran ahead, shoving people out of my way. At the intersection, I pushed my way into the tiny vortex that had collected around her.

She lay near the bus's huge front wheel, staring at the sky. One leg was bent, as though she were sunning herself at the beach. The pant leg of the other knee was severely torn, the visible skin gashed and bleeding, a bone sticking out. She had most likely been catapulted from her seat, smashing into the bus.

I knelt down. Her face was unmarked, save a thin red line across the bridge of her nose. I tucked my hand beneath her head so that the back of my hand felt the street grit and my palm held the bloody mess of hair.

"Darling," she said. "What happened?"

"There was an accident," I said, lacking the strength to say anything else.

"I'm scared."

She slipped her fingers into mine.

"Instruct me on my way," she whispered.

"I don't know how," I confessed. "But you're going to be fine."

She had never harmed or killed anything. She had, through perseverance and obstinate faith, remained true to her Buddhism and to her smiling Buddha. When the ambulance arrived, the attendant gave her an injection, and on the way to the hospital he fitted an oxygen mask over her mouth.

Throughout the ride her hand remained in mine. The fine bones of her fingers like the fine bones in her face were frail. Her grip was strong, her eyes half closed. I buried my head against her arm and prayed. Within the time one wishes for salvation, to replay a moment lost in time, or to redo what cannot be undone, her hand went limp and her breathing stopped. The attendant pushed me aside, pushed off the oxygen mask, and performed CPR. Between breaths, as he pushed down on her chest, he shouted in Thai to the driver to hurry up, *lai-o, lai-o*. Refusing to let her go, I slapped at her hand as if to waken her from a drugged sleep. I shouted her name; she didn't stir. Minutes before we reached the hospital, the attendant ceased his work. Melinda's face was calm, her mouth open as if prepared to speak.

The ambulance siren ceased. Within moments, I no longer knew her. I let go of her hand. It's true the story some people tell about gazing upon a familiar corpse and not recognizing the person. The woman before me was no longer the woman I loved. In my heart, I needed to believe this fantasy. The body I craved to be close to each night was vacant and deflated.

The ambulance bounced on the old road. Melinda's hand flopped off the gurney and hung down. I didn't touch it. The truth is, I couldn't bring myself to hold her hand again. I wanted nothing from her now.

A brain hemorrhage, the doctor would later explain to me at the hospital, was the cause of Melinda's death.

The next morning was the Buddhist holiday Visakha Puja Day, a public holiday commemorating the birth, death, and enlightenment of the Lord

Buddha. The dead could not be cremated until sunset the following evening. In addition, I had difficulty finding a *wat* and a monk to perform the cremation ceremony. Everyone was booked up, and I was told I would have to wait several days. To make matters worse, the day after Melinda's demise the hospital informed me they could no longer hold her remains, for they were cramped for space. I had a frightful vision of renting a taxi and hauling her in a plastic tarp to my hotel and holding court in the hotel room, talking to her corpse propped in a corner, smoldering and stinking in the Bangkok heat.

Tell me, what's the difference between carpenters and popes, refugees and presidents, thieves and mothers in death? The world had come unhinged. After leaving the hospital, I remember weeping in the taxi on the way to my hotel and the searing look of the driver in the rearview mirror. I suppose few Westerners wept in his cab.

The following afternoon, through the kindness of a hospital attendant, I was told of a facility on the outskirts of Bangkok that would allow me to store Melinda's body in a refrigerated space. When I investigated further I found the cost enormous. I went as far as to bribe the facility's representative, but knowing I was a foreigner, and believing I was rich, he refused to budge off his price. I would have tried another facility and would have used a Thai to negotiate for me, and bribed him as well, but I had to move forward with the arrangements. Finally, I acquiesced and paid the exorbitant amount. The company transported her to the facility for an additional fee. What did it matter? The woman wasn't Melinda, the one laid out so perfectly, if not elegantly, in her favorite blue dress, in the cold storage facility. I told myself it didn't matter how I disposed of the body. It wasn't Melinda anyway, and once you're gone who really cares except those who remember?

Two days later, I buried Melinda in a Christian cemetery in an outer Bangkok province. I supplied the casket, opting for something refined instead of the wooden pallet the grave diggers used for incarcerating the bodies of the poor and mendicant. I was glad I didn't have to choose a tombstone. This way it seemed she was more alive. Nothing blocked her way from re-entering my life, no stone or tiny palace. She had a vehicle back to this world. A vanishing, childlike part of me still refused to acknowledge her death. I knew this wasn't the way Melinda looked upon life and death. The burial was a selfish action on my part. She had wanted to be cremated, and I hoped she would forgive me.

Her few paltry possessions I would send on to her godparents in Hong Kong. I held back some items of clothing, her wristwatch, which I thought I would deliver someday to her son, if I ever discovered his whereabouts.

And what will I tell him, I wondered, as I left the cemetery on that clarion day and wandered into downtown Bangkok after a long taxi ride. If I found him and spoke to him years later when he had become a young man he would probably stare blankly at me and ask questions I would have few answers to. What was she like? Do I look like her? What happened to her? How did she die? I would have no definite response except some worn-out clichés and sweeping generalities that he would listen to intently, no doubt igniting fresh questions and proposals. He would sit before me, a slender young man, with eyes reminiscent of his mother. In the still afternoon air, I would want to lean forward and somehow seize the gene of her he held inside him. Nonetheless, my answers, I was confident, would leave him disappointed and with the same despairing look that had haunted Melinda. How could I tell her son that I still loved his mother and that I never fully knew her and had, in some offhanded way, been responsible for her death.

CHAPTER 29

THAT EVENING, AFTER a beer at Delaney's Pub, I went into Patpong. I wanted to feel the cold neon, see the whores, the touts, the girlie bars, smell the aroma of the food stalls, the grilled chicken and bowls of hot shark fin soup and walk in the open-air markets. I wanted to overload my senses and fill the deadness inside me with excess. Like Robert Mitchum in a grade-B movie, I was working hard to forget. I told myself not to think of Melinda, and I was ridding myself of the cemetery's fresh-air smell, the saccharine scent of burning incense sticks, and the endless Thai names on those tombstones that left my tongue confused. Now, there was one name I knew in that cemeteryland, and the whole country was cursed for me.

On the street the touts were active, as usual. They stood tempting customers with sex show menus on a square of cardboard. With slashing grins, they motioned to the upstairs club where one could see bugles blown from between girl's open thighs, the Ping-Pong show, a string of flowers or razor blades pulled from vaginas, or sex on stage.

In the large alley, amid the girlie bars, bright lights illuminated the evening outdoor market.

I walked through the busy marketplace. The scene was thick with sweat, tourist's money, and snappy-talking touts. Foreigners shuffled through the narrow lanes from stall to stall. From one of the vending stalls, I stopped and looked into an open-air bar and saw two boys Muay Thai boxing in a professional ring. A group of Bangkok's notorious ladyboys sat on the steps to the bar in tight sleeveless dresses, lightweight scarves wrapped about their throats, their faces painted with makeup.

Weary of the touts and tourists, I left the market and sat at one of the outdoor bars in the next alley and ordered a beer. A Sylvester Stallone movie played on a television screen in all its charismatic violence. Cars and motorbikes passed in the tiny road behind me.

The bartender brought over my beer.

"What's your name?" she asked.

"Herbert," I said. "And yours?"

"Me-ow." She smiled, and collected the eighty baht I had placed on the bar. "What work you do?" she asked.

"I sell and find things," I said.

"What you mean things?"

"Dolls, vases, trophies, possessions of the past."

"Oh, that."

She shrugged. I was just another loopy *farang*.

"One more beer?" she asked.

I nodded. The day's heat had not abated, and the beer had gone down without protest. She retrieved a cold Singha beer from a cooler. One of the street girls strolled over and asked me to buy her a drink. I refused. Unperturbed, she stroked my back and I pushed her hand away.

"What? Don't like girl?" she asked, dropping her hands onto her hips in a confrontational attitude.

"Not tonight."

"*By lao*," the bartender said to the girl.

I appreciated the bartender's professionalism, as she spoke in Thai, fending off the girl who strolled over to another customer.

"I don't want trouble," I said.

"That's okay," said Me-ow. "You want to be by yourself. Up to you."

Overhead, a door opened and loud rock 'n' roll music drowned out the television noise. I glanced up and to my right. A woman exited the upstairs bar and went to the iron rail that overlooked the street. She was thinly robed, and a breeze parted the slit dress, showing her thigh and hip. For a minute she stood looking up and down the narrow street.

She waved at a girl on a motorbike. Then, slowly, as if she were alone on a summer day, she descended barefoot on the metal stairs.

She took the stool beside mine. She had a plump, powdered face that hid her age. Her hand touched my sleeve, hung on my arm, and I knew the words before they left her mouth, the broken English that I had once found enchanting but now, like the pretty whores who filled these bars, ceased to charm me.

"What's your name?" she asked me.

"Sam," I said.

I don't know why I told her my true name when I had wanted to be invisible, cloak myself in a different persona, as if it were possible to ignore one's shadow. For many years I had been a trader in antiquities, dope peddler, merchant to rubes and fools, husband, and lover. I had worn many men's clothes, and I realized how deception had cost me all I cherished. I had forgotten most of the faces I swindled. Now I wanted to remember everything.

"What's your name?" I asked.

"Wat."

"Huh?"

"Wat's my name."

"Oh. Your name is Wat."

She smiled. "You're sad. Come with me."

I paid my tab and followed her up a flight of stairs. The skinny touts saluted me. The noise and hustle of Patpong fell away. She took my hand and it felt good to be led, taken without reserve, even though I knew what to expect, the lurid show. I was thankful. I would not have to care this evening; I did not want to care.

At our booth, Wat motioned for a waitress. Around her throat hung a single gold chain with an amulet and the engraved picture of King Rama V on its gold surface. She slid closer. In the dusky lighting, her makeup no longer existed. Her heavily drawn eyebrows softened, and the powder line on her throat melted away. Her chin, perfectly formed with a tiny cleft, rested against my shoulder. She had small ears, a wide nose, and eyes that revealed little.

The waitress served our drinks, a small glass of beer and a shot size glass of Cola for Wat. I held her name in my brain. Surprisingly, the spell that she had cast on me, which had lured me upstairs, did not deteriorate. She reminded me of a miniature Buddha, gentle and serene. It was only when she spoke *"Like a massage, sir?"* and her hand flopped on my thigh and a finger poked my balls did she break the spell.

On stage, a girl kissed another girl's breasts. Wat rubbed my leg, and I noticed a thumbsize smudge on Wat's chin, a birthmark that altered the prettiness of her face.

"Friend," Wat said, gesturing at one of the girls on stage. She took my hand in hers. "I speak little English," she said. *"Nitnoi."*

"Okay."

"I go now."

"Wait," I said, but she departed, leaving her drink untouched.

Almost instantly another girl filled the empty seat. Her shoulder rubbed against mine, and a finger playfully scratched my arm. She pointed at the Cola.

"Wat's," I said.

"No. Buy me drink, handsome man."

I looked across the bar and jerked a finger at a distant door.

"My girl," I said. "She went through that door. She come back. Soon."

I tapped the glass edge. I belonged to her. There was something so simplistically correct in the idea that I laughed. I smiled and laughed, nearing hysteria.

"My girl," I howled. I tugged the homely girl's chin, but she withdrew from me. I rubbed my belly, easing the fit. "It's really funny," I said to her. "My girl."

The dancer sulked, slumping against the vinyl cushion. I stared at the stage. The lesbian act had exited. Any moment Wat would return and place her tiny face near mine. Tonight I would explore her body, and afterward she would cradle me in her arms the way the grave's blackness did Melinda, and I would feel the same emptiness my lover occupied. The thought held no comfort. I drained Wat's warm Cola and wondered, *What suit of clothes is this?*

The stage lights dimmed. Over the microphone, a man announced the next event in Thai. The girl remained beside me, arms crossed, her eyes canvassing the bar for fresh customers.

Wat looked no different than before as she strolled between tables, chin lifted, the strange frown, a young girl from a distant Isaan province. She climbed the stage stairs and a sulfurous light showered her from head to toe. She stepped out of her toga. The light changed and her naked body paled. Beside her right foot was a bucket, and inside the bucket a foot-long stick which Wat gripped with the severity of a conductor's baton. With a lighter, she lit the stick's thicker end and watched it burst into flames. She tilted her head back and opened her mouth. Gradually, she lowered the flaming tip into her mouth, where it remained for a second or two. She pulled it out and presented the glowing stick to the customers.

She bowed, and with the tip pointed at the ceiling, Wat went to her knees and leaned backward until her lower backbone touched the heels of her feet. Her skin now seemed chalk white beneath the spotlight. Her other hand, palm down on the floor, steadied her body. Rotating her wrist, the stick descended, and when the flame was within inches of her face she plunged it inside her mouth. Her lips closed, and her arm trembled. I recall I was the sole patron who applauded. She grimaced, and seconds later she removed the stick's extinguished flame.

Sliding her legs out, Wat sat on the floor, lotus-style, and relit the stick. It was as though I had to remind myself she was naked. Her nakedness seemed as transparent as light, as if she were a window I could see through. Next, she lay on the floor with her knees partially bent, her legs spread.

She lowered the burning tip past her belly to her dark mound. A moment later tiny puffs of flame blew upward. She did this three times, releasing air from inside her.

The applause was slight. A customer threw an ice cube on stage. It skidded between her legs. A long-haired boy was shouting something in English in a strong German accent and had to be subdued by his friend.

Wat doused the stick in the bucket. She retrieved her toga and left the stage, following the same path she had entered, taking the same door.

"Buy me drink now," the girl beside me said. "Wat my friend."

"I buy only for Wat."

The girl left and went to sit with the two Germans.

I waited for Wat and reordered a Cola. Shortly, Wat squeezed against me, unsmiling, and sipped her Cola. It was only when she said the words, pay bar, and looked at me that I realized the discoloration on her chin was a burn. Perhaps some evenings, stoned or careless, her accuracy failed her. I pointed at the mark.

"Hurt," she said and looked away.

I touched her elbow. Gently, as if the Cola contained 101-proof rum, she swooned against me, her head resting on my shoulder. I reached into my pocket, threw some baht on the table, and watched her fingers dance among the red bills.

"This good," she said, grabbing the amount she wanted, more than the five hundred baht the bar required, and went off to pay the mama-san.

She returned in ten minutes dressed in a man's shirt that hung over her skirt, a vest, and wearing lime-green shoes. I paid the bill. As we exited, her fingers circled my arm.

On the street, the touts ignored us. Their mission had been completed. I hailed a taxi and told the driver my hotel.

"Wat," I said, "you are very beautiful," and afterward I remained silent.

As we traveled slowly on congested streets whose names I knew by heart, I felt like an outcast in a city I had stayed in cumulatively for months over the years. In the hotel room, I switched on the light and closed the drapes.

"I shower," Wat said, and went into the bathroom.

I stripped, tossed my clothes onto a chair, and stood in front of the full-length mirror attached to the closet door. It was the first time I had looked at myself unclothed before a mirror in a great while. I wasn't shocked or dismayed by the body reflected. I did not wish for one of those body types displayed in magazines of muscular men in string briefs, oiled and shaven, bodies that had never known excess or hunger or a fight. I stood three feet from the mirror and wondered how this body, still strong and fit about the chest but growing soft around the middle, had loved so few, and how fortunate I had been to be loved. I stared and stared; and finally Melinda appeared. As I gazed at the reflection, I saw her as clearly as if she had separated magically from my chest and now stood beside me. I was not overcome with emotion, but I felt the deepening sadness that comes over one who sees value in love, that most intimate experience, no matter how long or short in one's life, and accepts the experience wholly.

Melinda did not speak and, to be honest, I could barely make out the features of her face or her body. I knew, though, it was she, yes, and I tried to imagine her voice, the feel of her skin, and if I looked I would find one of Melinda's black hairs nestled on my arm, as I had observed before. But nothing survived of her save some trinkets, and the memory of her, of course.

A moment later, Wat walked by, smelling of Thai soap, breaking the trance. I knew the image I had conjured up was precisely that, as make believe as Melinda's Buddhist God, the one I had tried while Melinda was alive to love.

From the mirror, I watched Wat settle on the bed with the white towel wrapped about her body. Her hair was damp. She had switched on the television, the sound low.

"Do you have a baby?" I asked.

She smiled and shrugged. I put my arms together and rocked them imitating the cradling of an imaginary infant.

"Baby. Yes. No more. Dead."

"Husband?" I asked. "Are you married?"

"Thai man. No more married. No good."

It was enough talk. She propped a pillow beneath her head, totally absorbed in the Thai television program. The makeup had been washed away, and the absent lipstick disclosed a small mouth. I sat down on the bed and pulled open her towel. She was darker than Melinda. Her flat, muscled belly had the texture of hard butter. A butterfly, the size of a silver dollar, was tattooed to her hip. A few straight hairs covered her groin.

I snapped the light off and stretched out beside her. Exhausted, I dozed and was awakened by Wat as she twisted and punched at the air in her own slumber.

I shook her awake. "What's wrong?" I asked, pulling the blanket over us. "You cold?"

Her eyes opened. She shifted her back to me, her buttocks against my hip, and the cool soles of her feet on my calf. I slept for what seemed like seconds and awoke when Wat left my side, stepping out of the bed.

She walked soundlessly on the carpet. She passed before the live television, the black-and-white flowing patterns on the walls and ceiling, coloring the room in stormy light. Standing before the bureau where my canvas pack rested, I heard the zipper peeled from one end to the other, the hard cloth pulled back. From my angle, I could see her profile and the opened bag.

She carefully went through my things, examining each item, clothes, pens, postcards, opening a book and looking at the strange language, running her fingers over the black-ink words. Her hand moved through the folded layers of a silk batik. She opened another book and sniffed a pressed pink flower. Cautiously, she undid the seal to a plastic bag. She removed Melinda's watch from the bag, a slender gold band and a simple clock face. She held the watch in her open palm just below her breasts. I believed I could hear the ticking mechanism, as though someone had placed it to my ear. I rotated my head to get a better view. Unaware of me, Wat gazed at the watch now positioned close to one eye. The ticking appeared to grow louder. It was as though the watch hands had become a fuse and the battery, no larger than a fingertip, the explosives. Her thumb rubbed the crystal. I breathed deeply. She folded the gold straps around the clock face and, as she lowered her hands and brought the wristwatch toward her, I knew her belly was the detonator and all that I had loved was lost.

I shot out of bed, charged the bureau, and spun her forcefully around. There was no explosion, no rending of skin, only Wat's wails. She would not have taken the watch, and if she had, what of it? I knew it was only curiosity that prompted her fingers to fondle Melinda's watch and rummage through my pack. She crumpled to the floor crying, this girl who breathed and ate fire. Curled in the corner, she raised her hands before her face, fearful, I assumed, that I might strike her. I didn't know what to do. I took the blanket from the bed and draped it over her shaking body.

Sitting on the bed, the sheet drawn to my waist, I began to sing a lullaby. I sang in a voice that had often pleased Melinda.

Summertime and the living is easy
Fish are jumpin' and the cotton is high
Your Daddy's rich and your Mama's good lookin'
So hush pretty baby don't you cry

Wat's tears slowed. I wrapped a towel around my waist and retrieved her clothes. I dressed her, stitch by stitch, her underwear, skirt, blouse, and vest. On my knees, I helped her into her shoes.

I fished Melinda's watch out from under the bed where Wat had flung it. She stood, rolling the shirt sleeves to her elbow. I removed my wristwatch and gave it to her.

"Man's," she said reverently, taking it with both hands.

She pressed her palms together below her chin, the Buddhist way, and *wai-ed*. After securing my watch on her wrist, she asked for a tip. I picked my pants off the chair, dipped into a pocket and handed her one thousand Thai baht. She was a bright girl.

"You take me back," she said.

"No. Go yourself."

"You," she insisted. "Take me back."

"Okay."

I dressed as she combed her hair before the full-length mirror.

Outside, as I went to hail a cab, Wat stood on the sidewalk pouting, her arms folded across her chest, her chin dimpled.

"Where are you from?" she asked as I returned, luckless. We began to walk.

I hesitated and said, "America."

"Oh."

She placed her hand in mine. It gave her great joy to do this, I think, stroll hand in hand with a man from America. At a corner, Wat hailed a *tuc-tuc* and we jumped in.

We arrived in Patpong amid a downpour and stood huddled beneath a vendor's awning. When the rain shower slowed, we went toward the marketplace. Wat walked ahead of me, running her fingers through her damp hair. She strode past a crippled beggar, anxious, it appeared, to return.

At the outdoor bar, a lone customer sat drinking while the girl beside him ate pistachio nuts. It was two o'clock in the morning. The rain had slackened to a drizzle.

"You fast man," Me-ow said as I settled on a stool and watched Wat climb the metal steps to the upstairs bar in her bare feet, the lime-green shoes held in one hand, and not a word spoken to me. I caught a final glimpse of her, the small face hardening as she ascended the last rungs, the face of a queen in her lair.

I tapped the bar.

"Beer, please."

Me-ow delivered a Singha. "What now?" she asked.

CHAPTER 30

Two DAYS LATER, I arrived in Hong Kong. The monsoon rains were over, leaving a vibrant green on the tree-lined avenues and a morning melancholy in the air that lingered beneath the eaves of restaurants and stores. Once inside my apartment I found the place to be the same, though a bit mustier. I parted the curtains and opened the living room window. A harsh light streamed in through the glass porch doors in the rear of the room. I heard the sound of barking dogs chained to outdoor posts. The street noise of cars and buses and small engine motorbikes rushed by the window in brief, passing surges. I dropped my canvas bag on the floor. It settled, bending to one side, finally slouching to the ground until it lay flat. I remained standing; the familiarity was comforting. The tarnished tea pot on the stove, my bicycle and golf clubs in the corner, stacks of musical recordings, and rows of books told me this was home. I observed a block of brittle sunlight edge onto my desk. The three hundred-year-old jade dragon I had bought in Malacca, and my other artifacts, remained undisturbed. I stepped away from my bag, which was dusty and torn from the journey, and waited for some motion. There was none. Restless, I settled briefly on the couch, went through an archway to the bedroom, and sat uneasily on the corner of the bed. Uncertain of where to stay, I returned to the main room and sat on the floor, my shoulders to the wall and the canvas bag near my feet.

There, I watched the sunlight weaken, cross the floor and walls, touch the hairs on my arm, and recede. I listened to the noises of the neighborhood: Cantonese being spoken by strangers, the boy next door, my landlady's grandson running up and down the hallway. The wall pipes rattled.

In the downstairs apartment, someone was showering. I tried not think of Melinda, but she was here, though she had stayed but a few nights in these rooms. For so long I had kept her beauty inside me, and now that she was gone I could only pray *Melinda, come back and live with me for twenty, thirty, or forty years, for the rest of our lives.*

For weeks after my return, I revisited the places we had dined, the hotels we had slept at and made love. I wrote letters to an old address she once lived in. There was never an answer.

On stormy nights, unable to sleep, I often left my bed, flung back the curtains and opened the window. The night was always dazzling, as lightning bolts creased the black sky and the rain dashed against my face. I would sink back onto the bed, my body damp from rain and sweat, resurrected with desire and anticipation. For hours afterward I smelled Melinda, the scent of her hair and arms, the hollow of her spine that led to her small, round hips, and I was filled with joy. This revelation, however, was temporary. Shortly, this sensory illusion deserted me.

Nowadays, months later, the Mongkok dealers hang closed signs when I appear. Their rudeness is a part of my failure in Bangkok. And Lily, though generous in her serving of tea and sandwiches, does not engage my services. One botched assignment among this crowd and I am not to be trusted. Hence, I no longer deal in antiquities; my books are my only ally. Even the Liu brothers Zhi and Yi, avoid me. There's something distrustful in my eyes, the rumors say. The days are lengthy. Each morning I speak to my landlady until she coughs fitfully and breaks away. On wrong telephone numbers, I ply question after question to the caller in Cantonese, not wishing to release the unknown voice. I ride buses and converse with strangers, often young Asian girls who nod and flee at my discourse. In the evening, I sit in Victoria Park and speak to the phantom Melinda, even though I know she can't hear a word. I am not a Buddhist and do not believe in an afterlife.

Made in the USA
Lexington, KY
19 January 2017